solace 2

the final cut

k.l. hall

copyright

Solace II

K.L. Hall

dedication

To the Readers,

You asked, I delivered.
Enjoy.

-K.L. Hall

synopsis

The continuation of two wild hearts yielding to a fiery, soul-fusing, back-breaking love.

sol·ace

Definition:

a source of comfort or consolation

one

. . .

Six months later.

CASSIDY

From the tall fir tree decorated with bright white lights and a mixture of black and gold ornaments, to the Santa red stockings for Hendrix and I hanging from the mantel over my gas fireplace, my 1,200 square-foot apartment was *almost* ready for Christmas, and it was only a week after Thanksgiving. TLC's *Sleigh Ride* blasted throughout the apartment as I sat in the lotus position with my knees spread butterfly-style on the living room carpet, finger-fucking myself to Hendrix via FaceTime.

"Oh shit. That's it right there, baby. Yessss," I moaned, pleasuring myself faster and harder.

I pushed the pads of my feet together while tightening and releasing my pelvis and putting pressure on my G-spot. My fingers experimented with different patterns and rhythms as he talked his shit.

"Mmm, gush all over those fingers for daddy. Get 'em nice and wet for me."

He'd been coaching me through one mind blowing muscle contraction after the other for the past sixteen minutes and forty-two seconds, and he showed no signs of stopping.

I squirmed, tossing my head back against the plush couch as my next orgasm washed over me. "Ooooh shiiiiiiiittttttt!"

"Soak that shit up, baby," Hendrix's baritone voice hummed through the other side of the phone.

I slowly opened my eyes to take in the views of the mountain through my floor-to-ceiling windows in the living room, while trying to bring my heartrate down to a resting level. "Mmm, shit. I squirted," I announced, tears fogging my vision.

"You know I'm gon' break that back when I see you again, right?" he confirmed.

I ducked my chin in agreement. "Yes, baby. I can't wait."

The moment we stepped off the island, photos of us surfaced when we arrived at the airport hand-in-hand. Suddenly, I'd gone from a fly on the wall to bloggers wanting to know each and everything about me. So naturally, I resisted him, *hard*. Within ninety days, I'd gone from fighting Hendrix tooth and nail on all the laundry list of reasons why a long-distance relationship would never work, to giving him the spare key to my apartment for when he'd fly in to visit and break me off. We'd been going strong ever since. Falling head over heels with the creature with the whiskey-colored eyes and MVD *(most valuable dick)* was never part of the plan. Yet, it was safe to say Hendrix and I were more than just an interlude. He'd awakened something inside me. Something I'd never felt before with any other man I'd dated, let alone fucked.

For the past six months, we'd been splitting our time between my condo in San Jose and his spot in Kansas City. He stayed true to his word and let me decide how fast or slow I wanted things to go between us. Not once had he pressured me to permanently close the gap and come to him, and I appreciated it more than he knew. I loved my place, and I enjoyed my space. There was something about step-ping into my sacred space and closing out the world for however long I needed to that I craved. I enjoyed walking downtown to restaurants or visiting the farmer's market on early Saturday mornings. I had no intentions on giving up the heated pool and world-class gym I paid for every month to move halfway across the country and fold my life into his anytime soon.

I ran my fingertips along the back of the couch as I made my way back to my bedroom to finish getting dressed. Hendrix had lucked-up that he'd caught me fresh out of the shower with a towel on when we decided to have a little virtual afternoon quickie, but I had moves to make and people to see. I pressed the button to close the retractable drapes across the floor-to-ceiling windows inside my bedroom, closing out the view of the city and the garland and white Christmas lights wrapped around the railing on my private balcony. I grinned to myself, momentarily hypnotized by the twinkling lights until the annoying hum of the air conditioning brought me right back down to earth.

"Ugh," I groaned before dropping my towel on the floor.

"What's wrong?"

"Baby, it's December, and it's like sixty degrees outside. I don't want to spend another Christmas like this. For the first time in maybe ever, I actually want a fun, old-fashioned Christmas, okay?"

"And what exactly is an 'old fashioned Christmas'?" he asked, while bending his fingers in air quotes.

"You know, a Christmas where the heat kicks on inside the house instead of the A/C. Or dare I say even a white Christmas?"

"Sounds like you need to move out here with me then. I know for sure they gotta get snow out this mothafucka. I got a hoodie on right now and it's the beginning of December."

My shoulders shrugged. "Maybe I do," I said as my feet swept across the wide-plank wood floors from my bedroom to the kitchen.

Natural light flooded through my entire condo as I fished through the bowl of leftover Halloween candy on the quartz countertop. My eyes continued downward, zeroing in on the strawberry-flavored Fruit by the Foot as my lips danced around a smile.

"What are you cheesing about over there?"

"Oh, you saw that?" I asked, momentarily forgetting we were still on FaceTime.

"Yeah, I did."

"It's nothing. Don't worry about it," I said, changing the subject. "I have to get ready to meet Lauryn so we can do some more shopping for decorations for her baby shower. It's less than a month away, and she wants to buy up the damn store."

"Yeah, Mark was telling me about that. It's a little girl, right?"

"Yeah. You know her and Donovan just bought that house in Oakland. I told her I'd come over and help her unpack her decorations and make the house a home before we go shopping since she's all big and pregnant and not wanting to do shit."

"So you gon' go save the day, huh?"

I swiped my purse, keys, and box of decorations off the island and headed for the door. "You know me. But listen, I'm already late and you know how traffic can be, so I really gotta split."

"Okay, I'll let you go."

"Never let me go," I said, feeling myself turn to mush as the words fell past my lips.

"I'll never do no crazy shit like that," he confirmed before his killer smile sprang across his face.

I giggled. "Good. Bye, bae."

"Bye," he replied before ending the call.

———

One *Ashanti Essentials* Apple Music playlist, bumper-to-bumper traffic, and a grocery run later, I pulled up to Lauryn and Donovan's two-story home bearing gifts.

"Merry Christmas!" I beamed as soon as Lauryn swung open the door.

"It's not Christmas yet, Cass. Calm your holly jolly ass down." She chuckled.

"Well, ho-ho-ho to you too, *bitch*." I ushered a few steps into the foyer and gave the place a once-over. "Wow… where is your Christmas cheer? There's practically nothing in here."

"Did you forget we *just* moved here like a month ago? You were the one telling me that you were gonna come over, help me unpack, and sprinkle your little elf magic everywhere."

"Yeah, and trust me, I will. We can get you some stockings hung over your fireplace for you, Donovan, and even one for the little baby boo on the way. We can get you some holiday throw pillows for the couch and get you some lights and some more decorations for the tree for us to decorate."

Lauryn's face switched to a frown. I loved my girl, but I had the feeling that out of the two of us, I was the only one hype about the holidays. "Fuck Christmas, Cass. All I wanna know is did you bring what I told you to bring?" she fussed.

I held up the grocery bag with a pint of Ben and Jerry's *Netflix and Chilled* ice cream and a fresh bottle of Pinot Grigio for me. "Yes, damn."

"Good. You may proceed to enter the rest of the house," she pinged back, turning to lead us to the kitchen.

"Why thank you. Now, let me see this tree," I suggested, charging forward to the living room. When my eyes landed on the skinny, artificial tree tilted to its left side, I frowned. "This is it?"

She smacked her bow-shaped lips. "Shit, you lucky we got a damn fake-ass tree for you to decorate. With the stress of this move and having to pee every five seconds, I am not in the Christmas spirit."

"Oh, you ain't got to tell me. I can see it all on your grill. But don't worry, I got some decorations in the car, and I'm about to bless you with my Christmas magic. Let me go back out to the car and get the box of decorations."

I spun on my heels and walked back out to get the plastic, green tub of decorations filled with garland, ornaments, stockings, holiday knick-knacks, and more. Lauryn took one look inside the tub and shook her head.

"You don't think you're overdoing it?" she asked.

"No, why?"

"Can I be honest?"

I huffed before sitting the tub down. "Yeah, sure."

"I love you with every beat of my heart, but your obsession with Christmas is too damn much. You're like a little holiday whore with a nice ass."

I cracked a half-smile before looking back at my booty. "I know, right."

"I already know your ass got a Christmas tree in the living room by the window and another tabletop one in the kitchen. You probably got one in your bedroom too!"

I rolled my eyes to the sky. "And don't forget the big wreath on the outside of my door and the countdown calendar on my kitchen island that counts down the days 'til Christmas, and the garland on top of all my kitchen cabinets! It ain't no secret that Christmas is my favorite holiday! I'm loud and proud with mine!"

The two of us stalked over to the bare tree, and I started putting up ornaments and stringing lights while she sat Indian style on the couch with her ice cream in hand. Lauryn wore a half-smile as she indulged in the sweet treat, but I'd known her too long not to be able to see through the bullshit. Pregnant or not, she was eating her feelings. There was something on her heart that she wasn't talking about, and I wasn't going to stop until I found out what it was.

"What's going on with you, Lauryn? You good?"

She pulled the large spoon out of her mouth before shaking her head. "Nothin'. I'm fine."

"Everything good with you and D?"

"We're good, too."

"So, what am I missin'?" I queried.

She frowned. "Meaning what?"

"Meaning, how long are you going to lie to me and tell me everything is sweet when I can smell the bullshit?"

She hissed out a breath. "I just want to be happy, permanently. I want us all to be happy."

"Is there such thing as permanent happiness, Lauryn?"

She shrugged her lean shoulders. "I don't know. Every time I feel like I get a glimpse of it, it's always snatched away."

"What do you not have to be happy about? You just bought a house, you're engaged, and you're having a baby with the man you love."

"It's everything I thought I wanted. And don't get me wrong, I want it. I really do. I just—I just can't help but feel like the other shoe is going to drop at any minute. Like, what did I do that was so good to deserve all of this?"

"It sounds like you're dealing with some imposter syndrome issues. You deserve every good thing that's coming to you in this world, okay? You're a great person, Lauryn. You're gorgeous. You're smart. You're funny. You're—"

"Okay, okay. I get it. I don't know. I think I'm just nervous. Like what if this baby comes out and like never sleeps or rips my body apart on its way out? I swear, I be having the craziest thoughts run through my head all hours of the day and night, and I don't ever say anything to anybody."

"Why haven't you talked to D about how you're feeling?" I wondered.

She shook her head. "No. I don't want him to think I can't handle this, and I definitely don't want him breathing down my neck any more than he already is. I love him, and I don't want to put any more pressure on him."

"I understand, but you can't go around harboring all of these emotions either. You know I'm always here if you want to talk."

"Thank you, girl. Now, enough about me and my boring, pregnant life. Tell me all about this relationship with Hendrix. What's the tea? What's the update? You've been very private with this one, and I'm utterly shocked."

I shot up an inquisitive eyebrow. "Oh yeah? And why is that?"

"Because you're you, and I'm me. We share everything, bitch. You know, Mark can't get anything out of Hendrix either."

I snickered. "You just shaking all the trees, huh?"

"Every last branch," she joked, amusement rippling past her lips.

My cheeks flamed at the thought of him. "I don't know, Lauryn. It's just different with him. I don't know if it's because we have a past or what, but I'm...dare I say, happy?"

She cheesed, showing a full rack of teeth. "That's exactly what you should be if he's doing his job correctly, and from the looks of it, he is. You haven't stopped smiling since you got here. I know I'm cute and all, but I figured only D could have a bitch cheesing and showing all thirty-two like you are. So, go ahead and tell me about this perfect little secret love life of yours!"

"Hmph. It's good. We're good. We're, you know, taking it…day by day, month by month," I said coyly.

"Do I hear wedding bells?"

"You must mean your own, because…"

A frown shadowed her smile. "Because what?"

"Because we've only been together for a few months," I reminded her.

"Have you even thought about it?"

"Of course, I have. Every woman thinks of that, right? I'm not trying to get hung up on that. Relationships aren't always about having a piece of metal wrapped around my finger. No offense."

She shook her head. "None taken."

"I'm just saying, I like where we are right now and if a ring is in my future, then I'll cross that bridge when I get to it."

Truthfully, I'd been floating on cloud ninety-nine for the past six months. Shit had been better than good. It was the first time I admitted out loud that I'd entertained the idea of changing my last name to Croft a time or two, but I was still going to play it cool.

"That's it? That's all you're going to fucking give me? I've been patient with your ass for six whole months, Cass! So, no! Nah! You gotta give it up and you gotta do it right the fuck now, or I ain't puttin' up another damn Christmas nothin' in this house!"

I tried my best to stifle a smile. "I got everything that I want right now, trust me. You don't have to worry about Hendrix. He's taking good care of me," I told her.

She eyed me closely. "Mmm, physically or is he breakin' you off with more than just dick?"

I clicked my teeth together. "What do you mean?"

"You over here talkin' like he feedin' your soul and shit, so I just wanna know what else he's putting down other than pipe."

"I don't know why you think just because of his occupation, I'm living in the lap of luxury. I have my own and you know that."

"Yeah, I do. That's the best part! It's exactly what makes your fuckin' life so good. Stash yours and spend his!"

"Listen, before getting with Hendrix, I thought being the girlfriend of an NBA player was about the wining a dining, random vacations on a Wednesday, the shoes, *God the shoes*, you know? But now that I'm in it, being with someone that everyone worships is far from easy. For one, his schedule is crazy. He plays like eighty or something games a year. Half are in Kansas City and the other half are away and across the country. Sometimes he's gone for a couple days, sometimes he's gone for a week. And with my work schedule fluctuating the way it does, I can only really count on seeing him maybe one or two days out of the month."

"Oh, so you delirious from lack of the hood wood, huh?"

"Very. My dick supply is almost fully depleted, and my pussy is on life support. And trust, the phone sex ain't cuttin' it."

"Girl, I bet. Can't nothin' compare to the real thang," she boasted, spooning another mouthful of ice cream between her lips.

"Girl, and that's what I'm saying. My real thang is across the country at any given moment. These bitches swear they know more about my man than I do! They know his stats, all the teams he's played for, where he's staying, how long he gon' be there, everything."

"See, I'd have to cut a bitch. But you know, you wanna protect your peace and shit, like your face wasn't already in the blogs when those pictures were posted of y'all holding hands at the airport leaving the island like y'all was all in love and shit." She snickered.

"Yeah, but there hasn't been much talk about it since. We've been cautious. Mainly me, because I don't want or need all my business in the streets at any given time."

"So, the reason y'all aren't public all day every day is because of you?"

"Exactly. I told him I wanted to take things slow and that's what we've been doing. Just taking things day by day and month by month, like I said," I repeated.

We'd managed to keep the buzz to a minimum over the months, never confirming or denying anything. We'd order in instead of dining out and staying secluded behind the walls of his place or mine. We weren't posting all our whereabouts on the 'Gram, because the only two people who *needed* to know about us, knew.

"You a better one than me, that's all I'm sayin'."

"I'm not above it, trust. And don't get me wrong, it definitely bothers me sometimes because I know how scandalous some of these women are, but at the same time, these past six months have been so blissful because we've been lowkey for the most part. I enjoy a little tea and drama like the next bitch, but not when it's about me and the dick I'm sittin' on. I like my peace. I got my life and he has his. I don't wanna get swallowed up in him just because I'm dating him."

"Yeah, I feel you. I know I'd still be wanting to put these hoes in check, though. Belly and all," she reassured me, rubbing her round belly.

"I can't quit my life for him, but I still support him by watching every game on TV and cheering him on from the comfort of my eating sweats and couch."

"What the fuck did I tell you about them pants, hoe? Damn! Christmas is coming up, I'ma get you right. Say less."

I chuckled. "You're a bitch."

"And you still love me," she concluded, blowing me a kiss.

———

Two and a half hours later, I looked around Lauryn's house, admiring my work with a grin of satisfaction painted across my face. "Wow…"

"What?"

"It's beginning to look a lot like…"

"Christmas!" she answered, hanging the last few ornaments on the tree. "I still can't believe I let you do all this. I knew for sure we'd be at the store at least an hour ago!"

"Admit it! It makes you smile, right?"

"Yeah, it does. It'll be something nice to come home to. I guess you do know how to make a house a home or whatever," she said before rolling her eyes.

"I mean, it's nothing like my house, but we can't all be number one," I boasted as a chuckle blew from my nose.

"Now that we've done what you wanted to do, let's go do what I wanna do! Let's go blow a bag at the party store for my baby shower because everything has to be perfect! Oh, and let's stop by the mall so I can get a cinnamon pretzel and a pretzel dog with cheese!"

"Aight, let's go!" I chuckled before walking over to help her slide her swollen feet into her fuzzy black UGG slides and strolled out to the car.

two

. . .

HENDRIX

There used to be only three things I needed in life to be happy: money, basketball, and my freedom. In the blink of an eye, Cassidy had suddenly taken precedence over my need for freedom, and I didn't put up a fight about it. After seeing her again and spending the week with her on that island, I knew fate had stepped in and expedited our feelings for one another. When I got back, I made up my mind that I was done with all the nonsense that came with being single. I wanted her to be mine. Cassidy was the type of woman that made a nigga flex his brain. Everything about her made me want to go harder. I never expected to ever want to move mountains for her fine, stubborn ass. Yet, life was just better with her.

"How'd the interview go, babe?" I asked as soon as I answered her phone call, making sure not to answer her FaceTime call before having her call me regularly.

"Why didn't you answer my FaceTime call?" she inquired.

"I'm just leaving practice and my service is shitty. Tell me how the interview went," I said, changing my question into a statement.

"Not so good," she admitted.

"What do you mean? Walk me through it. What did they ask and what did you say?"

"They asked everything I thought they would. You know like, which programming languages and software I knew, and asked if I was ready to lead a team. Everything we went over."

"Okay, so what was so bad about it?"

"I don't know why I feel like I bombed it, but I do. You know how you can just catch a vibe when you walk into a room? I didn't get a good feeling. It was like they already had their mind made up on who they wanted for the promotion and interviewing me was just them checking the box."

"Did they say anything at the end, like when you could expect to hear something?"

She let out a frustrated breath. "They said they'd *be in touch*. That's never a good sign."

"Don't feel that way, baby. Just think positive."

"How about you think positive, and I'll continue to think how I think," she replied, tone dry as a bone.

"Or you could look at yourself in the mirror and see what I see."

"And what exactly do you see?" she probed.

"I see a woman who knows how to make a man pay attention. Look at what you've already accomplished. All you do is inspire. These hoe ass execs gon' hate and make you feel like you ain't on their level, but they need to get on yours. With a face like that and that gorgeous smile, plus brains—you a triple threat. I'm your number one fan, Cass. You a real one. I know it and you know it too."

I could hear her cheesing through the phone. "Thank you, baby."

"You know I always want to see you smiling and at your best."

"I know. I miss you."

A smile walked up one side of my face. "I miss you, too. Where you at?"

"On my way home. I stopped by the store to get a bottle of wine and some roll-ups."

"What you got planned when you get in the house?"

"I'm going to pop the cork on this lovely bottle of Pinot and take a nice, warm bath, and I'm definitely going to roll myself a blunt."

"It's been that type of day, huh?"

Her exhale gusted into the receiver. "Yeah, it really has, baby."

"I wish I could see you and make it all better."

"You on top of me would be goals right now," she confessed.

I kept her on the line until I heard keys jingling in the lock and stood to my feet. She opened the door to a trail of bright red rose petals leading from the front door all the way down the hall to her bedroom. Dozens of candles aligned her floor-to-ceiling windows, illuminating the view of city lights in her living room.

"What's that you said about goals?" I asked, holding the phone in one hand and a bouquet of long-stemmed red roses in the other.

She looked at me in awe before dropping her phone inside her Louis Vuitton bag. "Hendrix? W—what are you doing here?"

"I've been waiting on you."

"I can see that. And not that I'm not happy to see you, but *why* are you here?"

"I came to celebrate with you," I explained, walking over and presenting her with the roses before pulling her into my tattoo-laced arms.

She encircled my neck with her arms. "Celebrate what? I didn't get the job yet. It was just the interview, remember?"

"So what?"

"I can't believe you came all this way to surprise me. You've got rose petals and candles."

"And I got some rosé on ice and even got you a blunt rolled. You can get as high as you want tonight, baby."

Her eyes galloped up to mine as her lips swooped to one side. "You thought of everything, huh?"

"I think so."

"I still can't believe you're here," she chirped, running her hand down the side of my face. "You don't know how much I missed you."

"I could hear it in your voice earlier in the week that you were stressing about today, so I wanted to make sure I came to you and realigned your chakras and shit." I smirked.

I scooped her into my arms and carried her down the hallway and into the bathroom where I had a warm bubble bath and her blunt waiting for her. I sat her on the edge of the bathtub and slid off her heels one by one before rubbing the soles of her feet.

She dropped her head back and opened her mouth. "Mmm. That feels so, so good, baby," she groaned.

"There's more where that came from when you get out. Go ahead and take your bath, smoke, and unwind. I'll be waiting for you in the room whenever you're ready," I told her before gently kissing her lips.

———

Forty-five minutes later, Cassidy stepped out of the bathroom wrapped in her oversized towel with a set of hazy eyes and a demure grin across her face. I had songs by Maxwell, Daniel Caesar, Ginuwine, Jhene Aiko, and Trey Songz on the playlist to set the mood as I stood by the massage table I had set up in the corner of her bedroom.

"Hendrix!" she said, eyeing the massage table. "You really went all out, didn't you?"

I shrugged it off, knowing I'd never put that much effort into one woman before. "This is lightwork."

She batted her eyes at me. "Mmhm. Whatever."

"I just have one rule before you lay your fine ass on this table."

"And what's that?"

"No clothes allowed."

She willingly dropped her towel and laid across the table so I could oil her body down and massage her from her crown to the soles of her feet. After lathering my hands with oil, I embraced her curves while gently kneading her honey brown skin.

"You know, I was ready to write this entire week off, but you really turned it around for me," she acknowledged with her face buried in the table opening.

"See, all you needed was me," I affirmed, leaning down to place a trail of kisses down her spine. "I know that you've been missing me on you. Don't worry, daddy gon' give you all you can take tonight. Get your beautiful ass on the bed."

Cassidy tip-toed over to the bed and pressed her back against her lavender silk sheets. She flashed me a gentle grin as I encircled her waist in my arms and crushed my body into hers. "I wanna taste it tonight, Cass. No reservations," I said while shifting my bottom lip between my teeth.

"You know you don't need an invitation," she confirmed, spreading her soft legs from east to west.

I let my hands roam all over her body as if it was my first time touching her. I planted open-mouth kisses across the length of her slim waistline, and she squirmed. The second my lips touched her smooth skin, her body shivered.

"Ooh yes, baby," she moaned.

I rested the palms of my hands underneath the bend of her knees as Cassidy held my head hostage between her thighs as my tongue went into overdrive on her sweet spot. I reached up and grabbed her breasts as she dangled her legs on my shoulders. I glanced up at her and watched her suck on her fingertip and then run a ring around her nipples, getting them wetter and harder. I loved the euphoric faces she made. She was the portrait of beauty. Just watching her made my dick hard enough to bust through a concrete wall. I pulled her to the edge of the bed and flipped her petite body upside down to start eating her ass while she aggressively grabbed my dick with both hands. She felt my hardness grow through my boxers and didn't hesitate to pull it out. Her mouth lathered it up with spit, then sucked on my balls as the head of my dick rested on top of her shoulder.

"Open wide, baby," I mumbled to her.

She took my dick inside her warm mouth and sucked me off in the sixty-nine position.

"Take your hands off it, girl. You know how I like it."

Cassidy let her hands hang freely as I smacked her ass and thrusted my dick in and out of her mouth. As much as I enjoyed the foreplay, I was ready to be inside her. I laid her back down on the bed and started to climb on top of her when she reached out her hand to stop me.

"Hold up."

Confused, I asked, "What's wrong?"

"Nothing is wrong. I just want to try something new."

"Okay."

"Just lay back. I'll be right back," she told me.

I did as told with a grin across my face. Sex with Cassidy was always fire. She kept getting freakier and freakier as we went along. She popped out of the closet with a silk blindfold in hand and proceeded to blindfold me. Minutes later, I felt her warm hand grip my dick before feeling something cold and waxy being wrapped around it.

"Yo, Cass."

"Shh. Just go with it."

"What are you doing?" I probed.

"You trust me, don't you?"

"I do, but—"

"Okay, then. Now relax. I'll tell you when you can look."

That was the last thing I heard before feeling her warm mouth locked around my shit. "Mmm, shit," I groaned, palming the back of her head.

The harder she sucked, the more I could smell the sweet scent of strawberries, and the more curious I got. "Mmm. Let me look at you. You know I love lookin' at that sexy ass mouth wrapped around my dick."

She came up for air long enough to tell me I could pull off the blindfold before going back to work. I looked down to see Cassidy sucking my dick with a Fruit by the Foot wrapped around the length of my dick.

"You taste so fuckin' good," she groaned before flicking her tongue across the head.

"Goddamn. You tryna make me buss one before I beat it up?"

"No. Save it all for me," she told me.

I closed my eyes as she kept stroking my head with her tongue, picturing which position I'd beat the pussy up in first. "Come here," I commanded.

"Let me clean you off first," she told me.

She disappeared into the bathroom and came out moments later with a warm rag to clean all the stickiness off my dick.

"Where'd you get this idea?" I questioned.

"Remember that leftover Halloween candy I was eating a couple weeks ago? Yeah, well, I got curious and wondered what this strawberry flavored Fruit by the Foot would taste like wrapped around your dick."

"That shit felt good as hell."

"I figured it would."

"Now it's time for the main course," I said, getting up to pull her to the edge of the bed. With her knees pressed into her chest, we both watched my dick push inside her.

"Ooooh, fuckkkkkkkk," she moaned.

Her pussy locked around my dick as I slowly rolled my hips, digging deeper. Cassidy flashed her cat-shaped eyes up at me while biting her bottom lip. Everything about her was beautiful. I never thought I was a one-woman type of nigga until she came along. The deeper I fell in love with her, the wetter her pussy got for me. I tried my hardest not to slip up and put a baby in her, but if it happened, I wouldn't object.

"We should film this shit, baby," she announced.

Her statement caught me by surprise, but I was down for whatever with her. "Oh, you freaky, freaky, tonight huh?" I joked.

"Yes, baby. I want you to film me takin' it so I can watch us when you're gone."

"Say less. Where your phone at?" I questioned.

"In the living room."

By the time I propped up her iPhone at a good angle and flipped her over on all fours, Cassidy's pussy was drippin' like water. I grabbed the rounded curve of her hips and pulled her ass back toward me. I wrapped my hand around to massage her clit and get my thumb wet. I rubbed my thumb around her asshole and stuck it inside. Her body jerked forward as she panted like a thirsty dog with every stroke.

"Shit, baby!"

I smacked her ass as I watched her eyes roll back into her head. Cassidy's freshly manicured nails dug into the sheets as the muscles in her pussy contracted. Her body shook with bursts of pleasure then fell limp.

"Don't tell me you tired yet, baby," I said, still delivering one long, deep stroke after the other.

Cassidy laid flat on her stomach while I dug her pussy out from behind. My hand roamed through her scalp before I yanked a fist-full of hair. "Tell me it's all mine."

"It's all yours, Hendrix!"

"What's all mine?"

"T—this pussy."

"That pussy all mine, Cass?"

"Mmm, fuck! Yessss!"

"Get back up on them knees and throw it back for a nigga."

My eyes focused on the arch in her spine as she gently rolled her hips back toward my dick and bounced back against me.

"Yeah, that's what I like."

She had her ass propped up just right so that when I spread her ass cheeks apart, I could make her pussy crack a smile. The deeper I fucked her, the faster I felt myself nearing my climax. After a few more pumps, I exploded inside of her, and we both collapsed on the bed.

Once we caught our breaths, I slogged my way to the kitchen to get us both something to quench our thirsts. I walked back into the bedroom and saw Cassidy putting fresh sheets on the bed. "Might as well stop that shit right now."

"Stop what?"

"Making the bed. We ain't about to do shit but turn your bed back into an ocean anyway."

"Oh, really?" She smirked.

"Yeah, really. I plan to give you a round for every minute I spent away from you. I want that pussy drippin' like a sauna until I leave," I announced, gripping a handful of her ass.

———

"What time is it?" Cassidy inquired, rolling over to hook her leg around my waist.

"Six-thirty," I told her.

The sun had started to crown, and she had nothing on but a smile. I fucked her for hours until we both passed out on the plush, shag rug on her living room floor.

Cassidy sat up and started rolling herself a fresh blunt while I got up to sit behind her on the couch.

"You still coming to my game in Vegas on Christmas Eve?"

She tilted her head in a yes. "Yup. I will be there."

"Bet."

"How are you feeling going head-to-head against your old team?"

"As far as I'm concerned, it's just business. All I can do is go out on that court and give it my all like I do in every other game I play."

"Yeah, I know you'll be great. But um, speaking of Christmas, what do you want for Christmas?" she asked.

I chuckled. "I want you unwrapped and waiting for me under one of the many trees you got set up in here."

"You get that every time you see me minus the wrapping paper and Christmas trees." She chuckled.

"Nah, all jokes aside, I already got what I want."

"And what's that?"

I swiped her hair to the side before letting my lips collide with the nape of her neck. "You, woman."

She twisted her neck in my direction and clung her lips to mine. "Mmhm."

My hands found their way over her breasts as I slid my tongue in her mouth. She turned to wrap her arms around my tattooed neck before climbing off the floor and on top of me. The second I slid my middle finger into her sweet spot, the alarm went off on my phone.

"Fuck," I mumbled against her lips.

"Are you sure you have to go so early?" she whined.

"Visitation with my father is at nine o'clock. If I'm late, they won't make an exception. You know this is my first time seeing him in person since he's been doin' his time."

She nodded in agreeance. "Yeah, I know. I just hate seeing you leave."

"Me too, but I gotta jump in the shower really quick and get on the road. I'll see you again soon in Vegas for my game."

After getting out of the shower and getting dressed, I swiped up my bag and found Cassidy claiming a chair out on the balcony outside her bedroom.

"Aight, Cass, I'm about to be out. I love you," I revealed as I headed to her bedroom door.

The moment those last three words slipped off my lips, I curved my neck in her direction to see her face. She stared at me, doe-eyed and slightly confused.

A few seconds passed before she spoke up. "Hendrix, I—"

I shook my head. "It's cool, I'll wait. Don't trip."

"No," she said, grabbing both of my hands. "Don't say it like that. It's not that I—I just. I—"

"Cass, chill. I'm good."

A frown forged across her face. "Now I feel bad."

"Don't stress about it."

"How can you say that? I feel like I completely ruined the moment."

"If I said you good, then you good. Just know your heart is safe with me, Cass. You got everything I want. I ain't goin' nowhere," I guaranteed her. "But listen, I gotta go. I'll call you when my flight lands."

———

I left Cass wrapped in an oversized throw blanket and smoking a blunt on her private balcony while watching the sun completely rise. As much as I didn't want to leave her, I had to get on the road to start the drive up to Atwater to visit my father. U.S. Penitentiary Atwater was one of two high security prisons in the entire state. It was the first time he'd allowed me to be on his visitation list since he'd been locked up. He'd only write or call me, explaining how he didn't want my image of him to be behind a plexiglass wall.

I looked down at my console and saw a text from Cassidy pop up on the screen. *"You do know I care about you, right?"* she wrote.

I shook my head before quickly texting her back and turning my music up. *"I know,"* I wrote back.

She was holding back, but I didn't press it. Cassidy wasn't the type of woman who succumbed to pressure. I would much rather have her say it when she meant it, not because it was something she felt obligated to do. Drake's *Fair Trade*, blasted through my speakers as I put the thoughts of her to the back of my mind and focused on seeing my father live and in color for the first time in years.

I arrived at 8:30 a.m. to see the entire building perimeter behind electric fences, video surveillance cameras, and multiple armed guards at every turn. Once I filled out the paperwork and was processed by the guards, I was taken to a waiting area. They took me back for my visit forty-five minutes later, and I watched my Pops being escorted over to me by a guard.

I stood to greet him. "Hey, Pops."

"Prince," he said with a smile before pulling me into his arms and holding me for a few seconds.

I hadn't received a hug from my father since I'd left for college. He smelled like a fresh shower, so I knew he'd been diligent about his hygiene. He was in need of a haircut but looked like he'd been eating good and staying out the way.

"They treatin' you alright in here? You look good. Like you been hittin' them weights," I complimented, noticing his large biceps and bulging chest.

"Ain't shit else to do in here. And you know me, I'm straight. Half the gang in here with me, so I'm always good. Same shit goin' on out in the streets is going on in here. Murder, violence, and mayhem."

"You been thinkin' about what you wanna do when you get out? Last time we talked, you said you had about another ten before you were eligible for parole."

"They don't wanna see a nigga like me get out of here. I've already came to terms with the fact that I may never feel that warm Cali sun on my face again."

As depressing as his statement was, he was telling me the truth. He'd gone from being one of the biggest kingpins in Cali to just another inmate with a number on his wrist. "Damn, Pops. You can't think like that. Just keep doin' what you been doin' and you'll get out."

"Just in time to meet my grandkids, huh?"

I sucked my well-whitened teeth. "Grandkids? Where the fuck you get that from?"

He cheesed, showing a full grid of teeth. "I'm just sayin'."

"What you sayin', Pops?"

He shifted in his seat before changing subjects. "You know, I watch you on TV all the time. Niggas know what time it is when the king's son is ballin' on the tube."

"Yeah?"

"Hell yeah. You've been upsettin' niggas with these ass whoopings you've been handing out to these teams already this season. I tell niggas all the time, never go against a Croft man."

"Never," I agreed with him.

"You look good though, Prince. Life treating you well?"

I shrugged off his compliment. "I can't complain."

"You got somebody makin' you happy. I can see it in your smile."

"What you talkin' about, man?" I asked, refusing to look at him.

"I know that smile, Prince. Shit, I invented that smile. That's what good pussy does to you."

I chuckled. "Yo, chill, Pops."

"I'm just sayin'. Who is she?"

I sighed, not even able to downplay how I felt about her. "Her name is Cassidy. We know each other from back in the day. She lived in the same neighborhood as me and Moms after y'all divorced."

"You trust her?"

"I do. She knew me before the NBA and shit, and even back in high school she was never on my dick like the rest of them broads. She's got her own," I affirmed.

"Shit, if I ain't know no better it sound like you tryin' to put a ring on it."

My shoulders locked up for a second before I shrugged. "I don't know. Maybe I am. She's too bad not to wanna lock her down."

"And you ain't putting up a fight, huh?" he asked with a chuckle.

My grin softened into a genuine smile. "Nah. I'm ready for whatever."

He dipped his head in a nod. "Respect."

"Yeah."

"Besides your lady, what else is on your mind?"

"What do you mean?"

"I can tell you wanna say something to me, so go ahead and say what's on your mind."

"Aight, well, I wanna know what finally made you add me to your visitation list after all these years?"

"I told you, I never wanted you to see me like this. I wanted you to grow into the man that I raised you to be. I didn't want everything I'd instilled in you to be torn down by an image of me behind bars."

"Yeah, but it's not like I ain't know what you were doing out in the streets. You never hid that from me," I interjected.

"I know that, but when they raided my shit and tossed me in this hell hole, I couldn't allow you to see me reduced to this until I knew you'd found your place in the world. I didn't want my failure to hinder your success. You may not respect it or understand it now, but you will when you become a father."

My father and I talked for another two hours before the correctional officer told me we had ten minutes remaining in our visit.

"Damn, it's almost time for you to go already?" my father queried, sorrow in his voice.

"Yeah, I guess so. That hour went by fast, but I gotta get to the airport and catch my flight to Vegas. I'm playing in my old arena against my old team in a couple days on Christmas Eve."

"How you feel about that?"

My shoulders hunched forward. "I don't feel no way, really. A part of me is just ready to treat it like another game, but another part of me does feel a way. I won't say nervous, but it's something," I confessed.

"Didn't I tell you to stay focused and keep your head in the game? And look at you now. Just go out there and ball your heart out like you always do and give the mothafuckas hell," my father advised.

I bobbed my head while reaching out to dap him up. "You already know."

"Trust, I'll be watching you and cheering you on."

"I appreciate it, Pops."

He stood to his feet, pushing the steel chair away from him with the back of his legs. "Well, I ain't gon' hold you. Have a safe flight and take care of yourself out there."

"You take care of yourself in here, OG," I said, extending my hand to dap him up once more.

He swiped his calloused palm against mine and pulled me into a tight hug before tapping my back.

I turned to leave when I heard him call out, "Hey, son?"

I twisted my neck back in his direction. "Yeah?"

"If I don't see you, Merry Christmas."

I cracked a grin, knowing he wouldn't see me before Christmas, but I appreciated the lightheartedness of it just the same. "Merry Christmas to you too, Pops."

three

. . .

Christmas Eve

CASSIDY

The gold, tufted headboard knocked against the wall with a final thud as Hendrix climaxed. He'd broken his rule about no sex before a game and broke me off just a mere hour before he had to be at the arena. Since my flight had landed in Las Vegas, it had been nothing but one back-breaking escapade after another inside his room at Caesar's Palace.

"Shit," he groaned before rolling off me. "See what you made me do?"

I allowed the crisp, white bedsheets to swallow up my body. "Call it an early Christmas gift." I giggled while being thankful I'd remained faithful to my birth control.

"I gotta hit the shower. The bus will be here to start picking us up and taking us to the arena in half an hour," Hendrix announced.

"Maybe I'll just rewatch the porn we made and get myself off again if I get horny while you're gone," I teased.

He shook his head, reminiscing just as I was. "That shit was so fuckin' sexy, Cass."

"I know right. I've never done that before."

"Trust me, baby, you were a natural. The camera loved you. You can star in another sexy movie anytime you want."

"Yeah, yeah. You get one little movie role and now you know all about directing and shit, huh?" I joked.

"Yo, chill. What time are you coming to the arena? The game starts at six," he reminded me.

"Don't worry. I'll be getting dressed and heading over to the game in the next couple hours to cheer you on," I avowed.

"Good. It'll be good to know my lady is in the building."

"Are you sure you're ready for us to put the rumors to rest and officially go public? This will be the first game of yours I'm attending in person," I mentioned before taking a bite out of the leftover avocado toast I had delivered to the room for breakfast.

"I'm ready if you are. I don't want to do anything to make you uncomfortable," he answered.

I effortlessly grabbed my phone to begin swiping through my social feeds. My eyes landed on a clip of Angela Yee's Rumor Report on The Breakfast Club.

"*The blogs are all buzzing about a potential romance between NBA star Hendrix Croft and his co-star, Tamia Barker, after the two were spotted getting cozy after shooting a scene on set of their new movie, Undeniably You, where Croft plays Barker's ex,*" she reported.

I glanced up at Hendrix while trying my best not to let my insecurities run amuck. "Speaking of movies, you're a tabloid favorite as of late," I said, letting my uncertainties run right through my loose lips.

"Oh, that shit?"

"*Oh, that shit?*" I mocked him. "You ain't know you were secretly dating your co-star for that movie you got a couple lil' lines in?" I asked, waving my hand to downplay his accomplishment.

He sucked his teeth. "Oh, now it's just some lil' movie and shit, but when I first told you about it, your ass was all gassed talkin' 'bout *oh, bae, what am I gonna wear the night of the premiere? Blah, blah,*" he mocked in a high-pitch voice.

I rolled my eyes toward the ceiling. "Whatever! This is the shit I'm talkin' about though, Hendrix. I like the lowkey vibes we've got going on except for when I have to read about you in the blogs with someone else, knowing it's not true."

He slowly sauntered up behind me, kissed my neck, and started massaging my breasts through the sheets with a high thread count. "Having you at my game as my lady will put all that shit to rest, again, only if you're comfortable," he reiterated before pecking my rose-pink lips.

"I'm not uncomfortable," I confirmed. "Or at least I wasn't."

"If there's something you want to ask me, then you have to floor to do it," he asserted.

"Fine. I guess I just want to know if I should be concerned or not."

"No. It's just these dumb ass gossip bloggers our agents are paying to cooking up a story about us to generate buzz for the movie. That's it and that's all. She got a man and I got you. It's childish gossip. You're all I want. I promise you that. The only question now is do you believe me?"

I tipped my head forward. "I do. It's annoying because I was just talking to Lauryn about this shit a few weeks ago, and she was getting on me about us not being all out in the blogs and on the 'Gram and shit. I know for damn sure she won't shut up when she sees this shit on The Shade Room." I said, puffing air through my nostrils.

"Tell your girls you with a real one, so they can calm they asses down. We ain't gotta be postin' our every move on the 'Gram. We got our own thing going on, and we doin' shit how we wanna do it. I told you from the beginning, I'm just along for the ride with you. If you'd rather sit in the stands instead of with all the other player's wives and girls, I'm cool with that, too."

"Yeah, I'm not rushing to be the center of attention on anyone's blogs again, but I'm ready to do this with you. The timing feels right," I told him.

"I'm a firm believer that if it's real, then everything should be effortless, you know?"

"I completely agree, and I'm glad we're both on the same page," I said with an agreeing plunge of my chin.

"Just know I'm yours. Mentally, spiritually, and physically."

"And I'm yours. Now go get in the shower and get ready."

He pecked my lips once more before disappearing into the bathroom. Hendrix was my drug in human form. There was more between us than just the symphony of our bodies. Even after our bodies parted, my soul was still intertwined with his. I'd done things with him I'd never imagined doing with anyone, let alone someone in the limelight, and I didn't want anyone else.

Twenty minutes later, Hendrix's legs jolted in motion as he exited the bathroom in a cloud of steam with a towel wrapped around his waist.

"I want you waiting for me under the covers when I get back. I'm still feignin' for you, but I gotta get to the arena," he announced.

"I'll be at the game. And then I'll see you back here later."

"You promise?"

"Of course. I wouldn't miss waking up next to my favorite person on my favorite holiday."

Hendrix smiled to reveal his canines. "Bet." He swaggered over to kiss me goodbye, and I pulled him in for a deeper kiss. "You better stop before a nigga slip back inside you," he mumbled against my lips in his sexy, panty-dropping tone.

I pulled away from him and felt dizzy. "Okay, okay. Bye. Have a good game."

Hendrix left without telling me he loved me, and I didn't question it. He hadn't said it since the night he'd surprised me in my apartment, and I didn't say it back. Not saying it back still fucked with me because I *did* love him—it was one thing, but *saying it*? Saying it took on a whole new thing that I didn't know if I was ready for, even if my heart was.

————

Walking into the arena, I felt the tension and excitement coursing through the air. Hendrix had a point to prove to almost everyone under the roof, and I was glad I could be there to support him. Knowing I was there solely to support my man didn't help to put my own anxieties to rest when it came to taking my place in his world, but I trekked on accordingly.

The arena attendant scanned my mobile ticket and escorted me to the private VIP suite with the rest of the players' wives and girlfriends. From the looks of it, none of them had heard of a bad hair day or ever experienced a chip in their nail polish. Everything from their designer bags to their French-tipped toes being paraded around in designer shoes were flawless. I couldn't help but drag my eyes down to the outfit I'd chosen to wear. I had on a custom-fit jersey with Hendrix's name on the back, jeans with a Gucci belt wrapped around my waist, and my favorite pair of Christian Louboutin heels, yet I felt like I stuck out like a sore thumb and completely out of my element. I still felt awkward about going to his game alone and trying to play nice with women I didn't give two shits about, but I knew how to play the game. It was his workplace, and as an extension of him, I wanted to make sure I made a good first impression.

Bass-heavy music blared as the smell of freshly popped popcorn wafted past my nose. I grabbed the first available seat I could find and parked myself there, wishing I had my girls there to mix and mingle with so I could loosen up more quickly. I wasn't looking for new besties in the WAG community, but I also didn't want to come off stuck-up and reserved and end up causing more drama. It was hard for me to identify as anything or anyone but myself. Up until then, I'd been careful not to envelop my life into his, yet these women embodied high fashion, good looks, and flashy lifestyles I saw on reality shows. I didn't see how I fit into that.

"Here, have a glass of champagne," a young woman of mixed descent offered. "It'll knock the edge off."

I obliged with a smile. "Thanks."

"Is this your first time here?"

"That obvious, huh?"

She chuckled. "Just a little. I'm Tori," she introduced herself, extending her hand to mine. "I'm Keyshawn Randolph's wife."

"Nice to meet you. I'm Cassidy."

"Nice to meet you, too. Who are you here supporting?"

"Number twenty-two, Hendrix…"

"Croft?" she answered before I could finish.

"Yeah."

"So, how long have you two been dating?"

"I'm not sure that's any of your business," I replied, instinctively protecting my privacy.

"I'm sorry. I didn't mean to offend you, but some of the players bring girls up to the suites days after meeting them. You know, here one day, gone tomorrow type of flings."

"Hendrix and I are far from a *fling*," I assured her.

"Oh, good. I didn't get that vibe from you, but I just wanted to be sure."

"Sure of what?" I inquired.

"Just before I introduced you to the other women, of course. A lot of the players' girlfriends and fiancées have learned a lot from almost everyone in here. We're a mix of entrepreneurs, CEOs, models, mothers, and everything in between. We don't share the knowledge of the game with *one hit wonders*, as we call them."

I smiled at her gesture. "Again, I'm not a *one hit wonder*, or whatever you call it. Hendrix and I are together. No matter what you've read in the blogs or what you've heard, I'm his woman. I'm good on the knowledge but thank you though."

She nodded before letting out a harmless chuckle. "I get it. I was just like you when I first started coming to Keyshawn's games. Reserved, guarded. I thought I knew everything about my man and had all these other bitches on notice that I was his and he was mine, but it doesn't always matter to some."

She seemed to speak to me from past trauma and experience.

"This is just all...a lot," I acknowledged, taking in the sight lines across the arena.

"Oh, trust me, I get it. Some of the ladies can be very..."

"Intimidating?" I asked, finishing her sentence.

"I was going to say bitchy, but intimidating works too," she joked.

The two of us shared a gum-baring laugh. "Merry Christmas, by the way."

"Oh, thank you. Merry Christmas to you, too. It's been slipping my mind all day that it's actually Christmas Eve. When it's game day, nothing else really matters."

"Christmas is my favorite holiday."

"It used to be my favorite, too."

"Used to be?" I queried.

"Well, when the season starts, we're always here or there. I travel when he travels, so if we're lucky, we can spend Christmas at home, but more often than not, we're in some hotel suite somewhere, where it hardly ever snows. So, I kinda lost my love for the holiday over the years."

"Mmm, gotcha. Well, at least you get to spend it together, right?"

"Yeah, I guess you're right."

"How long have you been married, if you don't mind me asking?"

"No, I don't mind. We've been together for ten years and married for seven."

"Wow. Congratulations. Is it everything you'd thought it be?"

"Marriage or being the wife of somebody in the league?" she asked.

I shrugged before taking a sip of my champagne. "Both, I guess."

"It's definitely an adjustment, and with everybody thinking they know your every move, it can get annoying sometimes, but as long as you know who you married, or in your case, dating, then you gotta be able to overcome the bullshit if he's who you really want."

I gave her a warm smile. "Yeah, I'm not sure I'm ready for the lime-light and all that comes with it. Being famous was never something I wanted to be."

"He'll always be the famous one, honey, while some only see us as glorified groupies who lucked-up and got rings."

I nodded, appreciating the gems she dropped about her experience as a wife, and I tried my best not to let her get in my head. I knew damn well I was more than a glorified groupie.

"Well, the game is about to start. I'm going to get back over to my seat. You're more than welcome to come sit with me and a few of the other ladies if you want," she suggested.

"Thanks, but I think I'm going to kick it here for a while and watch the game. I might join you ladies at halftime though."

"Sure. Suit yourself. Enjoy the game."

Hendrix's sweat-sheened skin looked so good playing under the bright arena lights as the jumbotron camera zoomed in on him. He was on fire, dropping twenty points before the half. After a few more glasses of champagne, I'd loosened up enough to cheer him on out loud when he made a basket and move over to meet Tori's friends. By the middle of the third quarter, my feet hurt from jumping up every few seconds, and my voice had gone hoarse from chanting *defense* with all the other rowdy spouses in the suite. I was more than ready to head back to the hotel, shower, and wait in the bed for Hendrix like he'd asked. When I was too worn out to stand up, I scrolled through my news feed when my heart dropped to the soles of my yelping dogs. Suddenly, the posts on my feed had gone from hilarious photos of the Elf on the Shelf to photos of Hendrix and another woman flooding my timeline. I looked up and saw everyone's eyes focused on me, including Tori's.

She drifted over to me with a look that told me she already knew where my head was at from past experience. "Are you okay?"

"I—I gotta go," I stammered, realizing that wearing Hendrix's name across my back made me even more of a target.

Unable to hold my head and face the ridicule and embarrassing stares a second longer, I ducked out of the suite, pulled off the jersey, and tossed it in the first trash bin I could find before darting out of the arena before the game ended.

four

. . .

HENDRIX

We won the game 110 to 87, and I couldn't have been happier. I'd been riding the high of a three-game winning streak and coming out on the winning end against my old team had been icing on the cake. I figured the dip inside Cassidy I'd taken before the game was a good luck charm. On my way out of the arena, I pulled my phone out of my bag to call and ensure she was naked and in my bed as I'd requested. Before I could navigate to dial her number, I noticed I had several missed calls and unread texts. I instinctively knew something bad happened. In fact, I'd miscalculated how bad things were. It turned out the paparazzi had leaked photos of me with a woman outside of my hotel after an away game in Phoenix. The way the photos were angled, it looked like we were kissing, when in reality that couldn't have been further from the truth.

"Man, fuck!" I barked, ready to toss my phone in the trash.

I quickly called Cassidy and was sent straight to voicemail. Then, I called my agent, knowing I was possibly facing a PR disaster. Hours before Christmas, my face was splashed across every tabloid magazine and blog in the country over some shit that I knew looked worse than it was. I knew if Cassidy had gotten wind of it, she was going to be expecting an explanation.

When I got back to the room, all her things were gone. I pulled out my phone to call her over and over, leaving a slew of voicemails in my wake.

"You've reached Cassidy. Leave a message after the beep," her voice recording echoed through my speakerphone.

BEEP

"Cass? It's me. Answer your phone. Where are you? I'm in the room and all your shit is gone."

BEEP

"Listen, I know you probably have a million questions running through your head right now, let alone people in your ear. I just wanna talk, aight? Please, just call me back. Did you get another room? Just tell me where you are, and I'll come to you."

Anger seared my skin as I spent the next hour calling her while waiting for her to call me back. On what seemed like the hundredth time I'd called, she answered.

"What do you want?" she asked as if I was nothing but a nuisance to her.

A frown etched into the side of my mouth. "What the fuck you mean, what do I want? I wanna talk to you, Cass. I've been calling your ass non-stop for the past hour!"

"I don't have anything to say to you."

"Bullshit. Then, why aren't you here then? You just gon' up and leave me like that with no explanation or telling me where you at?"

"I'm a grown woman, and I can come and go as I please."

I shook my head, trying not to let her quick ass responses drag me down to her level. "Just tell me where you are, and I'll come to you."

"That's not necessary."

"Why isn't it? We need to talk."

"I don't want to see you."

"Cass, stop being stubborn and tell me where you are. Did you get your own room here in the hotel?"

"No."

"Did you get a room somewhere else on the strip?"

"No," she replied, just as dry as the first time.

I drew in an exasperated breath while pinching the bridge of my nose. "Then, tell me where you are."

"I'm at the airport, Hendrix."

My eyes bulged out before frosting over with anger. "The airport? What the fuck are you doing there? Come back to the hotel so we can talk, Cass."

"No. I'm going home, Hendrix. This whole thing was a—"

"A what? A mistake?"

"You said it, not me," she retorted.

I thrust out a breath. "Look, I already know you saw those whack ass photos, and before you go feeling a way, just let me explain. You at least owe me that."

She scoffed. "I don't owe you shit, nigga."

"Just up and leavin' like that with no explanation? You toxic as hell for that and you know it! How is it that the first time you hear or see something you don't like, and you up and leave me for the streets without even hearing my side?"

"Why do I need to hear your side of anything with the truth right here in my face? I don't have shit else to say to you, okay? Everything done in the dark comes to light, remember? And thanks to you I've got the whole fuckin' world in my business because of your lies!"

"Cass, just let me fuckin' explain. It's not what it looks like, I put that on everything I love."

"Oh, like how you love me, right? I don't believe shit that comes out of your lyin' ass face! Here I was trying to convince myself that I didn't need to wait for the other shoe to drop with your ass, and boom, here we are. You know what? I hope you and that two-dollar bitch have a merry fuckin' Christmas!" she snarled before hanging up in my face.

five

. . .

CASSIDY

I couldn't believe I was boarding a flight back home hours in advance of Christmas. I was surprised that the universe had obliged my wish and granted me the last seat on an outbound flight on Christmas Eve. I so desperately wanted to be sandwiched underneath the solace of my own sheets and completely close out the world, Hendrix included.

After hanging up on him, I put my phone on airplane mode ahead of boarding so I wouldn't have to be bothered with the million messages flooding my group chat with my girls. Each of them had sent me the screenshots of the photos separately and then all together in the chat. They each took turns analyzing every detail of every picture and questioning where I was, what was I going to do, and if I was okay. They all got ignored.

Truth be told, I didn't know what I was going to do or if I was okay about it. I couldn't believe I'd gotten hung up on every word that fell off his silver tongue. I'd been blinded by the dick and in my eyes, he could do no wrong, but the pictures were there in my face. One was of him walking out of his hotel with some mocha-colored, skinny bitch with long, dark hair. Another was of the two of them standing beside each other and talking, and the last was of her leaning up to kiss him. If it weren't for the last one, I probably would've excused the first two, but seeing another woman's lips on his—at what was reported to be booty-call hours—set a fire inside me that couldn't be extinguished. *You're smarter than all this shit, Cass. What the fuck were you thinking dating a fuckin' ball player?* I asked myself before resting my head in between my palms.

———

The moment my legs propelled me through my front door; the waterworks started to pour. I'd barely kept it together in the backseat of my Uber on the ride home. All I wanted to do was shut out the world for as long as I could. Glancing down at my phone, I noticed the clock had passed midnight and it was officially Christmas morning. For months, I'd fantasized about waking up on Christmas morning with Hendrix by my side. I'd look over at him sleeping peacefully, and I'd cherish the moment of our first Christmas together. I would've done anything to feel his arm slip around my waist and spend the day in isolation, opening gifts and watching holiday movie marathons. Yet, I was home alone with a suitcase full of tears, humiliation, and regret. Although it was Christmas, juicy gossip didn't sleep. I'd gone from a fly on the wall to having my name in everyone's mouths. I had to face the fact that Hendrix and I weren't on the island in our secluded villa. We were back to real life, and with real life came bullshit.

After I got out of the shower and washed the airport stench off me, I took my phone off airplane mode and prepared myself to face the music. I hadn't had my phone in hand for more than five minutes before it started vibrating.

"Lauryn, what are you doing up so late? Is everything okay with the baby?" I answered.

"Waiting for Santa. *Bitch*, what do you think? I needed to hear your voice to make sure you were okay! And yes, the baby is fine."

"Good, and I'm fine."

She smacked her lips. "Lie again."

"I mean, I think the three of you established that out of all the pictures posted, the one where it looks like he was kissin' that bitch was the icing on the cake, right? So, how do you think I feel?" I retorted.

"Have you spoken to him?" she asked, bypassing my defensive attitude.

"Barely. I'm not really in the mood to speak to anyone right now," I confirmed, hoping she'd show me some mercy and get off the phone without a fuss.

"I just needed to hear your voice. I know you're not okay, and that's okay. This love shit is hard. You know I'm always on your side, but I do think you should hear him out whenever you do feel like talking."

I shrugged. "Maybe. But it's late, and I just got in from a flight. I'm going to get some sleep," I said. My second attempt at trying to end our conversation before it headed in a direction I didn't have the energy for it to go.

"Hold up. Flight? You left him in Vegas? Is that why you haven't been answering any of our calls?"

An exasperated huff flew past my twisted lips before I responded, "You damn right I left his ass! You think I was gon' sit around in his hotel room and let him lie to my face?" I snapped.

"True. So that's it, though? You're done?"

My nose wrinkled at her question. "What do you mean? Yes, I'm— I."

"You don't have to know right now, Cass."

"I just...ugh! Seeing those photos triggered the fuck out of me. Especially after that shit with Omar, you know? I can't believe I got played again!"

"No, you're completely right. Getting played by a nigga is fuckin' traumatic. Trust, we've all been there and still got the PTSD to prove it. So, your feelings are valid."

"Things went from being so perfect hours ago and now, boom! I'm hit with this shit. There's a part of me that wants to hear him out, but there's a bigger part of me that saw the photos with my own two eyes. What more do I need him to explain to me? Obviously, he's been out here fucking other bitches, so there's nothing more to be said. I think I just need to put what's left of this relationship in my rearview and count my blessings it didn't get worse."

"If that's what you feel like you wanna do, then I support you. I just—never mind."

"What? Say it."

"I'm just sayin' that you don't have to be the superhero all the time, Cass. I don't want you to throw everything away so quickly. You said it yourself, he was making you happy, right?"

I rubbed the back of my neck as my phone dinged. There had been pictures of Hendrix and I linked to the pictures of him and that bitch with the headline *Who Really Has Hendrix's Heart?* I threw the phone down and buried my head in my pillow to let out a muffled scream. My life had turned into an episode of *The Bachelor* and dealing with the unwanted court of public opinion while trying to figure out my own shit, had me stressed to the brink.

"Cass? Cass! Are you okay? Answer me!" Lauryn yelled through the speaker.

I slowly picked up the phone. "I know what I said, but as you can imagine, my feelings have changed since then! I'm a fucking story all over again! These bloggers don't give a fuck about my real life, only what makes their click rates and impressions shoot through the roof. My love life, my mental health, and everything else are expendable to them!"

"Girl, fuck these bottom of the barrel-ass, scrounging through people's dirty laundry for some clout ass bloggers! As long as you two know what it is, then that's all that matters."

I exhaled. "Look, I know you're being my girl and checking in on me, but I seriously can't talk about this shit anymore. I—just need to shut out the fuckin' world and get some sleep, okay?"

Air left her nostrils in a huff. "Okay, goodnight, girl. Call me when you wake up, okay?"

"I told you, I'm fine. Don't worry about me. Enjoy your Christmas."

A sigh escaped her lips before she replied, "You too, Cass."

I quickly deaded the call before setting the security alarm and putting my phone on *Do Not Disturb* mode. My arms encircled my pillow as I pulled it tight to my chest. Falling all over myself in love had gotten me nowhere, once again.

After tossing and turning for much of the night, unable to save my thoughts from skydiving to conclusions, I finally drifted off to sleep. I shot up in the middle of my bed to the whirring of my alarm. Before I could even gather my thoughts, I heard a familiar voice yelling my name from the hallway.

"Yo, Cass—"

"Hendrix?" I asked, staring at him standing in the middle of my hallway, red-eyed and tired. Bypassing him, I quickly darted over to disarm the alarm. "It's like seven o'clock in the morning. W—what are you doing here?" I asked as soon as the alarm stopped.

"You tell me. You're the one who left me."

"So, you come here and break into my apartment in the middle of the night? You scared the shit out of me!"

"Breaking in? I have a key. A key that you gave me, remember? Besides, I tried knocking and you didn't answer."

"That's because I was asleep, and even if I was wide awake, I don't want to talk to you, let alone see you!"

"Please, Cass. I need you to hear me out. If you want me to leave after that, I'll do whatever you want. I just need you to listen."

As reluctant as I was to let him stay, let alone hear him out, I wouldn't have been able to live with myself knowing he was tired, and I'd turned him away. "Fine. Say what you came to say," I declared, bunching my arms against my chest to cover my hardening nipples.

The scent of his Dior cologne enveloped me in a mix of warm fields of amber and sun-drenched blue skies. Even though he was the last person I wanted to see, I couldn't take my eyes off him as he slowly sauntered into the living room. His usual military posture was hunched over, and his body was tucked in the left corner of the couch to ensure he kept his distance from where I stood.

"Well?" I inquired.

six

. . .

HENDRIX

Coming down from the high of the win against my old team and walking into an empty hotel room had me shootin' to Cassidy's crib like it was a drive-by. Being that it was the holidays, finding an available flight out of Vegas to San Jose wasn't an option, so I rented a car and drove eight hours to her front door, arriving there a little after seven o'clock Christmas morning. By the look on her face, she hadn't expected for me to show up in the flesh. She was used to the chase, and as much as I admired her, I wasn't going to spend the rest of my days running after someone who didn't eventually have plans on getting caught.

"Well?" she inquired, arching an accusing eyebrow.

"Do you promise you're gon' hear me out and listen?"

"Why would I promise you anything?" she asked, flashing her critical eyes at me.

"Because I drove over eight hours to see your ass, that's why."

Her brows squinched together. "I never asked you for any of that."

"And I didn't ask to come home on Christmas Eve to an empty hotel room with no explanation as to where you went."

Cassidy ambled over to the couch and stared at me while picking at the edge of her throw blanket with her fingertips. "Just tell me who the fuck she is. And you better not fuckin' lie to me."

"I don't know that bitch. I got the paparazzi on my head over some dumb shit when I don't even waste my time with none of these groupies."

"You act like you just became famous yesterday, Hendrix! You know they are always in your damn business, sniffing around for a story. I'm just mad I let you, let me play myself."

"Play yourself?"

"Yeah, that's what the fuck I said!" she spoke abrasively.

"I've never played you, Cass. Those photos were from the away game in Phoenix a few weeks ago. She was there with my teammate, Keyshawn, who had the room right next door to mine.

"Keyshawn like Keyshawn Randolph?" she interjected.

"Yeah."

She grunted. "Mmm."

"What?"

"I met his wife, Tori, at the game."

I shook my head. "I don't be in that man's business about what he does and who he does it with. All I'm worried about right now is me and you."

"And yet you still haven't explained how she ended up with you if she was with someone else. Or do y'all just pass bitches around like hot potatoes?" she assumed.

I sucked my teeth. It was clear she was irritated beyond the point of consoling because she let reckless shit fall off her lips. I needed to bring her ass down a few notches.

"Look, I know I'm not your favorite person right now, but—"

"But what?" she asked, rolling her neck before journeying into the kitchen.

I stepped up to her. "You ain't gon' keep talkin' to me like I'm fuckin' anybody. I been told your ass you need to do more listenin' than talkin', so sit your ass down and fuckin' listen for once!" my voice barked over hers.

Her eyes lit up in surprise that anyone would speak over her, let alone give her a command. Without saying another word, she posed her ill-mannered ass on the barstool at the kitchen island, rustling with the half-eaten cookie on the napkin in front of her.

"I need you to hear me, and I need you to hear me clear, aight? The bitch came knocking on my door at three o'clock in the morning because he got drunk and passed out, and she wanted to leave. Niggas ain't supposed to have nobody in their rooms, if so it's an automatic fine. She told me her phone was dead, so I called her ass an Uber and walked her down. When the car showed up, she turned to kiss my cheek to thank me and fuckin' left. I didn't know her ass then, and I don't know her now. I ain't been on no body but yours."

She sat with her lips pursed together in silence, refusing to offer up a response.

"Well?" I probed.

She shot me a glare that was cold as ice. "Oh, I can speak now?"

My lips twisted in anger. "I'm about two seconds from walkin' right the fuck outta here, Cass. Cut the bullshit, aight? I'm telling you the truth."

"And how am I supposed to believe you?"

"Because I haven't given you any reason not to. You're so caught up in your past traumas that you don't even know you're a part of the fuckin' problem! I understand you've been hurt, but you don't have to hurt me when I ain't done shit but be loyal to your ass. I told you to your face that I love you. You think I go around sayin' that shit to anybody?"

"Clearly, I don't know what you do when I'm not around."

My body tensed; I could feel myself seconds away from wanting to throw in the towel. "Even when I'm not around, you get all of my time. If it's not ball or some shit I gotta do to make money, then you have everything else. I've put you second to none for months! You think I curve these hoes every day because I don't want them? It would be easy for me to fuck, but I don't. I'll check any hoe if she cross the line because I ain't tryna jeopardize what we have. I haven't lied to you once. Why the fuck would I start now?"

"Because you got caught up with your side pocket!" she fired back, flapping her arms around in the air as she spat out her words.

"I swear to God, Cass, you really about to make me leave."

She raised her thick, arched right eyebrow. "Run me my key before you leave," she demanded while holding out her hand.

I scowled. "What? Really, Cass? You really gon' take it there?"

"Again, I didn't ask you to come here. You said you wanted to explain, and you did, so you know where the door is. I'm not stopping you."

"So, that's it? You done with me just like that?"

"You're the one who said you were leaving."

"But do you want me to go?"

She pulled in a tight breath and let it out slowly. "Look, Hendrix, I just think that—"

"What? What do you think? Because I ain't done shit but put you on a pedestal and you know it!"

"I did the same for you!"

"Then, why are you letting this go so easily?" I quizzed.

"Because I can't love someone like you!" she shouted. Her broken-hearted eyes continued downward toward the floor as she swept her finger against her mascara-straightened lashes to brush away the tears.

My brows sloped. "Someone like me? What the fuck is that supposed to mean?" Cassidy had a thing for acting off pure impulse. It was fine when it was used at the right place and time, and right then wasn't it. "Answer me!"

When she didn't respond for the second time, I made my way to the door while pulling the key to her apartment off my keyring. "Then, I guess there's nothing left to say then," I verified before stopping to place the key on her countertop and then slamming the door behind me.

I trekked halfway down the hallway to the elevator when she called out to stop me. "Wait, Hendrix. Come back! I'm sorry, okay? I didn't mean to say that, and I don't want you to leave. I guess, I just wanted to beat you to the punch. You know, to hurt you first," she admitted.

I turned and angled a glance down at her. "Why would you wanna hurt me?"

I could see the sadness in her tear-dampened eyes. "I—I don't. Well, I did, but not anymore. I'm sorry, this is just all so much for me, and I guess I'm not adjusting as well as I thought I was."

"Do you love me?"

A burst of air shot from her mouth before she drove her eyes down to the floor. "I do love you, I'm just—scared out of my fucking mind. Seeing those photos put me in the worst headspace, and I went into survival mode, okay? Learning how to maintain my sanity in your world is a lot, and I can't get my heart broken again." She quaked.

She tried hard to maintain her hard exterior shell, but all I saw was a scared little girl struggling with her own insecurities. Knowing I lacked patience for a lot of shit, Cassidy was someone I saw myself waiting for; in this lifetime or the next. "I told you that your heart was safe with me, didn't I?"

"Yeah, but—"

"But nothin', Cass. You already know where I stand, and it seems like I'm not the one that needs to figure out where they wanna be. You either wanna be with the me you know in your heart, or the me these dumb ass blogs are trying to make me out to be."

"I *do* want to be with you, but—"

"There should never be a but after you say somethin' that you mean, Cass. Why don't you get that? I love you, *but*. I wanna be with you, *but*. All this red light, green light, stop, go, slow down, stay, leave shit you doin' is childish, and I'm not on that type of time. And at the end of the day, the real flex is, this is the type of shit I was trying to be on with you," I fussed, digging into my pocket and pulling out a small gift box.

"What is that?"

"Your Christmas gift," I told her. "I planned to give it to you after the game, but you dipped out on me."

"Hendrix, I said I was—"

"Just open it," I told her. She took the box out of my hand and pulled the perfectly tied red satin bow apart. Inside was a key to the house I'd recently rented in Kansas City. "I was hoping you could make my new house a home, but I can see you not ready for that."

She raised the top of her nose to me. "Hendrix, listen. I—"

"Nah, you listen. I meant what I said about not letting you go, Cassidy, but I'm not doing this back-and-forth dance with your ass. I guess it was only a matter of time until something came along and tried to tear us apart, but I'm still fighting for this to be something. I don't want to be the only one fighting. So, how all this plays out is in your hands. I don't want to hear shit else from you right now. I want you to take some time and when you really figure out what it is you want, then you let me know," I declared.

"Can you at least just come back inside and get a couple of hours of sleep before you go?" she requested.

I shook my head. "Nah, I'm good."

"Hendrix, don't be like that."

"I told you I'm straight. Enjoy the rest of your Christmas, Cass," I told her before pressing the elevator button and stepping inside.

seven

. . .

CASSIDY

I'd barely made it through an hour and a half-long staff meeting at work before swiping up my Celine bag from behind my desk and skating off to lunch. I planned to spend the hour refueling with a much-needed meal and the largest cup of coffee I could get my hands on. A week had passed since my life blew up on Christmas, and the bloggers had finally moved on to another story. I finally felt free enough to walk outside my building without hiding my eyes behind oversized sunglasses or shielding my face with my hand. As I stood in the line at the Starbucks down the block from my company's building, my phone vibrated. Noticing it was coming from my office, I quickly rolled my eyes and braced myself for some unforeseen bullshit.

"This is Cassidy Stokes," I answered.

"Cassidy! It's Jacquelyn Warner from human resources. Is now a good time?"

"Y—yes," I answered hesitantly.

"Great. I wanted to let you know that you've been selected for the promotion to lead the operations division out of our new office in New York. Congratulations!"

My eyeballs popped wide as I struggled to push words out of my mouth. "T—thank you. But um, New York? I didn't know that was on the table. I thought I would be taking over the operations here in California if offered the job."

"Let me look over the interview notes here, just one second."

Her pregnant pause allowed me enough time to put her on mute and step up to the overworked, syrup-pumping barista to place my order. "Hi, can I get an iced venti caramel macchiato with seven pumps of caramel syrup, extra whip, and a hazelnut and mocha drizzle? Oh, and a chicken and bacon panini?" I requested before pulling out my card and swiping it in the machine.

"Ms. Stokes?" Jacqueline called out, back from doing her research.

"Yes, I'm still here," I answered after taking the phone off mute.

"Okay, it seems like there were interviewing for two positions that needed to be filled. One here, and one in our New York office. The interviewers were impressed with your background and felt you would be best to head the division in New York. Now, should you accept this position, the company will pay your relocation fees given that you do so in ninety days."

"Ninety days?" I repeated.

"Yes."

"Okay, and when would I need to give you an answer?"

"As soon as possible but seeing as though we've just come off the holidays, I'll say at least by the middle of next week. Will that work?"

"Yes, the middle of next week. Got it. I'll be in touch and thank you again for calling."

"No problem, congratulations again!"

I smiled so hard my cheek started to cramp as I savored the first slurp of my custom drink order. "Thank you."

The serendipitous call was the only thing able to put a pause on my downward spiral since things had ended so poorly between Hendrix and I on Christmas, no less. Hanging up and sucking down my custom-made drink order had suddenly made my day ten times better. I wanted to keep the good vibes pouring in and decided to call the one person I knew could keep a smile on my face.

"What up, floozy?" Lauryn answered with a childish giggle.

I quickly smacked my cherry red painted lips together before my smile returned. "I'm gon' let that slide because I have good news!"

"I like good news. What are we celebrating?"

"You remember the job I told you about? You know, the promotion I was interviewing for?"

"Yeah."

"Well, they called me like ten minutes ago and told me I got it! I still can't believe it because I swear to God, I thought I bombed that shit!"

"There you go, being all negative again. How many times I gotta tell you that you a bad ass bitch?"

I rolled my eyes to the bright, blue sky above me. "Yeah, yeah. You sound like—never mind," I disputed, stopping myself before I uttered his name.

I hadn't fully processed everything that had gone down between Hendrix and me. I'd finally confessed my love for him and still managed to let him slip right through the palms of my hands like putty. I must've stared at the set of keys in the gift box for an hour straight after Hendrix left that morning. A week had passed since then, and he hadn't asked for his keys back. Without knowing the address to his new home, I couldn't use them anyway, so I guess he rendered them useless in my possession.

My heels clicked and clacked across the pavement back to my office as Lauryn spoke up. "Speaking of him…have you heard from him? You know, since you told me about all that shit that went down when he showed up at your spot on Christmas?"

His words still floated around my head and messed with my scorned heart. He'd gone out of his way to explain himself to me. No other man had ever driven eight hours to explain himself to my face. The most I'd gotten was a text paragraph or Omar's sorry ass confession over a shared appetizer.

"We speak here and there, but it's not like it was. But listen, talking about him is really going to kill my vibe, and I'm havin' a pretty stellar day, so can we not?" I asked as I swiped my badge to get back inside the building.

"Okay, okay! I'm sorry! You're right. Fuck him! Back to the job.

C'mon and give me details! What's our new title? What are our responsibilities? And most importantly, what's that pay 'bout? Give me all the deets because I'm livin' vicariously through your ass while I'm locked down in the house on nesting mommy mode."

"I'd be the director of operations at the new office they're opening. So, that means I'll be doing the day-to-day stuff like making sure my employees are monitoring, alerting, and patching any software issues for the company. And the pay is…*divine*," I indulged.

Accepting that job would put me in another tax bracket, but I'd been a West Coast girl all my life and didn't know how I'd adjust to The Big Apple. A part of me felt like the job offer couldn't have come at a better time. The universe had seemingly delivered the sign I'd subconsciously been praying for. Maybe a fresh start in New York was exactly what I needed.

"Heyyyy! That's what the fuck I'm talkin' 'bout! My girl 'bout to be Cali paid in the Cali shade!" Lauryn cheered, prompting the bittersweet reminder that I hadn't spilled all the tea about where the job was actually located.

"About that…" I muttered before closing my office door behind me for privacy.

"What?"

"It's more like New York shade."

"Girl, what the hell are you talkin' about?"

"The job is in New York, Lauryn."

"Now what now?" she asked.

I heard the sadness in her voice, and I immediately found myself choking back tears. "I know it's not ideal, but…"

A whizz of air expelled from her lips. "No. No. The devil is not going to steal my joy today! This is a good thing! This is so, so good, Cass! You gotta do what you gotta do."

I bobbed my head before kicking off my heels behind my desk and taking the first bite out of my warm panini. "You're right, I know. It's like I know I should be excited and be jumping at the chance, but I don't know. California has always been my home. I don't know how I'll adapt to New York, let alone moving there in the cold."

"I get it, but it ain't nothin' to buy a winter coat. I bet you'd look cute in some fur," she joked.

I smacked my apple red lips at her. "Look, I've got another meeting to get to in like twenty minutes, and I need to finish my lunch. I'll talk to you later, okay?"

"Okay, we'll finish this conversation about this big opportunity this weekend at my baby shower."

"Yup, sure. I'll be there bright and early Saturday morning to help Shauna and Brielle with the decorations," I promised her.

"Okay, I'll talk to you later."

The moment I ended the call, I closed the door and started chowing down on what was left of my panini. Lauryn was right; the promotion was a good thing. As happy as I was to have a win to celebrate, it killed me not to be able to pick up the phone and tell the one person I wanted to share the news with. Everything outside of my love life seemed to be falling right in line. After savoring the last bite of my lunch, my phone vibrated against my cherrywood desk. I quickly flipped it over to see the name *Mom* written across the screen. Although my mom and I barely had what I would call a "good relationship," I'd been dodging her calls for a few weeks to prep for my interview. I didn't need her negative ass fuckin' up my headspace, but since the job was in the bag, I decided to pick up.

"Hey, Mom," I answered, slowly praying her response wouldn't make me want to hang up in her face.

"Well, if it isn't my long-lost daughter."

I let out a sigh-growl. "Sorry I haven't gotten around to calling you back. It's just things with work and everything have been a little crazy for the past few weeks."

"Last I heard from you was a *Merry Christmas* text at eleven o'clock at night. What's been going on? How's work?"

"A lot has been going on, and work is good. I actually have something to tell you."

"I have something to tell you, too, but you go first. What's your news?" she inquired.

"I got offered a new job, the director of operations at a new office my company is opening."

"Wow, director of operations. That's a strong title. It better come with the salary to match."

I pressed my lips together tightly, careful not to say the first thing that came to mind. I'd literally said five sentences to her, and she already had something critical to say. I didn't know why there was a part of me that still required her approval. I was a grown ass woman, yet I felt like I still wasn't good enough in her eyes. "It does," I confirmed.

"Good. I taught you well."

"Well, the thing is, I don't know if I'm going to take it," I confessed.

"Why wouldn't you take it, Cassidy?"

"Because it's in New York."

"Oh, wow."

"Yeah, and they said they'd pay for my relocation fees as long as I do so in the next ninety days."

"As much as I don't want you to be going all the way across the country, I do think this new job will be good to put some distance between you and that ball player that had your face all over the blogs. Who knows, maybe you'll meet my future son-in-law in New York."

My forehead creased. "Why are we even discussing Hendrix right now? This is about me. Besides, he's all the way in Kansas City and I'm here in Cali. I think we have enough distance between us as is."

"A little more wouldn't help," she suggested.

"What's that supposed to mean?"

"I'm just saying, never put all your eggs in one basket, and when I say basket, I'm talking about Hendrix, so there's no confusion. I mean, his mother is a prime example."

"His mother? Why are you talking about his mom?"

"It's the truth! She stuck by his drug dealing daddy all those years, and where did it get her? She's lucky her offspring can dribble a ball or else she would've been pushing cans on the side of the freeway years ago, mark my word." She snorted.

My mother was the type to think she was better than most of the people around her because she could put *doctor* before her name, and she'd never operated on anything or anyone in her life. Little did she know, I welcomed the distance the job would put between me and her the most. Her years of judgment and constant criticism were part of the reason I was so emotionally fucked-up in the first place.

My face scrunched up in disgust. "That's a horrible thing to say, Mom."

"Be that as it may, it's the God-honest truth. *You* are your priority, Cass. No man should come before that."

I glanced down at my watch. "You know what, Mom. I've got a meeting to get to, so I've gotta go."

"Wait, there's still something I need to tell you."

"Can we talk about it some other time, Mom? I really do have to go," I repeated.

She drove out a harsh sigh. "Yeah, sure. I'll talk to you about it some other time."

"Okay, thanks. Bye!" I barked before snappishly ending the call.

———

The weekend rolled around, and somehow, I'd still managed to be in a good mood. I'd even started looking at available rentals in the big city in my down time. The more I toyed with the idea of accepting the job and all that came with it, the more I saw myself spreading my wings in NYC. To ensure the day was all about making sure my best friend had everything she needed, I put my thoughts to the side and focused only on celebrating the new life that was created in nothing but authentic Black love.

I pulled up to Lauryn's house bright and early, happy to see that the weather was cooperating for her Pretty in Pink baby shower brunch. And trust, she'd gone all out for the special occasion as only she would. Various vendors had come in and transformed her back-yard into a lavish pink oasis. From the phenomenal balloon décor to the flower wall filled with various shades of pink roses, and the beautiful pink cabana, everyone invited was sure to have a great time. Both Lauryn and Donovan had successful careers and could afford to blow a bag on their baby girl, and I wasn't mad at it.

"Oh my God, this is so beautiful!" I cheered as I pulled Lauryn into a warm hug. "How are you feeling? Are you excited?"

Lauryn beamed as she grinned from ear to ear. Between the glow pregnancy had blessed her with and the utter happiness in her voice, I'd never seen her look more beautiful.

"I'm so in love with how everything turned out. Like, we're going to have a blast. The food truck should be here soon."

"What's on the menu again?" I asked.

"There will be chicken and waffles, French toast, shrimp and grits, uh—fried mac and cheese bites, and—"

"Damn, girl. It's cool. I get it, we gon' be eatin' good. And trust, I will be stuffing my plate with all the comfort food I can get my hands on. So, what do you need me to do? I'm here to work!"

"Brielle just got here like two seconds before you did, and Shauna is on her way, so you can go in the kitchen and help her with whatever," she instructed.

"I'm on it!"

I spent the rest of the morning tying pink bows around the mini rosé champagne bottles as to-go gifts for her guests. Once everything was perfect, the four of us did our makeup and got dressed.

"Okay, ladies. I must say, the coordination between the outfits is fire, okay!" I bellowed as I swooped my hair and edges up into a top knot bun and poked my oversized gold hoop earrings into my ears.

The four of us were all dressed in different shades of pink. Brielle wore a fuchsia pink off-the-shoulder top and matching wide leg pants set that complemented the fresh, honey blonde box braids she rocked. Shauna had on a blush lantern-sleeved dress that accentuated her mocha-colored curves in all the right places and stopped right past her knees. Adorning my body was a Christian Dior off-the-shoulder puff sleeve jumpsuit in the shade of baby pink, and the mommy-to-be rounded out our quartet with a hot pink pants suit with matching heels.

"Hell yeah! We look too good not to take a million pictures today," Shauna agreed.

"I'm so happy you all are here to celebrate my baby girl," Lauryn stated before instinctively rubbing her stomach.

Brielle jerked her chin in agreement. "Of course. You know there's no place else we'd rather be."

"Yeah, girl. We wouldn't miss this for the world."

"Exactly. That's what your girls are for, right?" I spoke up again. "Now, let's go enjoy this brunch!"

Since it was a co-ed baby shower, Lauryn and Donovan decided they didn't want to play any of the traditional baby shower games. Instead, we all spent the sunny afternoon dancing to good music, eating, and radiating good vibes only throughout the pink atmosphere.

"Um, can I have everyone's attention before y'all start heading out? Real quick, we just want to thank you all for coming to help us celebrate Bleu, who will be arriving soon," Donovan announced before reaching down to rub Lauryn's protruding belly.

"Some days my due date can't come fast enough," Lauryn interjected with a chuckle.

"Um, I think Lauryn and I have also decided to make a little announcement."

"Damn, you pregnant too, D?" Brielle blurted out before everyone broke up in a roar of laughter.

"Nah, I'ma leave the baby carrying to my *wife*. I just focus on making them," he replied with a chuckle.

We all fell silent for a few seconds before Lauryn spoke up to confirm that his mention of her being his wife wasn't a slip of the tongue. "That's right, y'all. Surprise, we got married!" she broadcasted before swiping happy tears out of her chestnut brown eyes.

My mouth dropped open, and I quickly sought out Brielle and Shauna's faces to see if they knew something I didn't. They looked just as dumbfounded as I did, so I turned my attention back to Lauryn, who refused to make eye contact with me for more than a couple seconds at a time.

"Surprise is right! Oh my God! Congratulations!" Brielle cheered.

Everyone else followed suit and soon the entire backyard was filled with cheering and clapping. "Thank you everyone for coming. Thank you all so much. We really do appreciate each one of you for taking some time out of your busy lives to be here with us. We hope you had an amazing time, and we will be sure to keep you posted on baby girl's arrival," Donovan said, wrapping up their speech.

Once people started to shuffle out, we each started taking gifts into the living room, stacking them mountain-high in the corner to be opened later. Then, the four of us were finally able to kick off our heels and huddle under the cabana to catch up.

"Okay, so when were you gon' tell any of us that you got married, bitch?" I asked, the first to speak up.

"I told all of you today."

"What made y'all want to go off and elope like that?" Brielle asked.

"Yeah, I thought you were excited about planning a big wedding," Shauna added.

Lauryn shook her head before swiping her long curls behind her ears. "I was until I got pregnant and realized how much work goes into planning a wedding. I didn't have the mental bandwidth to deal with that shit. So, we talked about it and we decided that we wanted to be married, period. So, we flew out to Vegas when I was about five months pregnant and eloped."

"You mean to tell me you've been secretly married to this man for months and didn't slip up once?" I asked, folding my arms across my chest in shock.

"Oh my God it was so hard, y'all. Like, you don't understand how bad I wanted to just blurt it out!"

"What did your parents say?" Shauna asked.

"You already know Mama and his mama were pissed when they found out, but, hey, we did what we felt was best for us."

"And fuck the rest!" Brielle chimed in before turning her mini champagne bottle up to her lips.

"Exactly. I've always hated that whole outdated ideology that we have to do things in a certain order or a certain way, like that first comes love, then comes marriage shit. Real love isn't a boardgame. I don't think any one thing has to happen first or last. If two people form a dope connection and have a mutual understanding of what it is, then that's all that matters. No matter how fast or slow that happens," I agreed, letting my thoughts wander back to Hendrix.

Shauna let out a deep, heavy negro spiritual sigh before waving her hand to the sky. "Well! Preach on!"

"Shit, well I'm happy for you, girl," Brielle chirped.

"Yeah, me too. If you both are happy and you feel like you made the moves you needed to make for your relationship, then there's nothing else to be said," I assured Lauryn.

"Yassss! Congratulations, Mrs. Mackey!" Shauna shouted before displaying a wide-gapped grin.

Lauryn's coppery-brown skin blushed a beet shade of red. "Thank you! After I drop this baby and lose all this baby weight, we plan on renewing our vows in a real intimate ceremony with our friends and family. I'll be able to drink then, so you already know we gon' be lit!"

"Yassss!" Brielle hailed before making her long, honey blonde box braids pop against her ass as she did a quick twerk.

"So what has been going on in your life, Cass?" Shauna asked, putting the spotlight on me.

"Yeah, what's up with you and Hendrix? Have you spoken to him?" Brielle inquired.

I shook my head with a huff. "Not really since Christmas. You know he told me his side of the story and then he told me to take some time and think about what I wanted, so that's what I'm doing. Now with this new job promotion on the table...I don't know what I'm going to do."

"Pause! Job promotion?" Shauna asked, folding her arms across her size DD chest.

"See! I ain't the only one that's been keepin' secrets!" Lauryn called out.

I rolled my eyes. "I literally just found out I got the job a few days ago. You kept your shit tight for months. It's not the same!"

Lauryn sucked her pearly white teeth. "Whatever."

"Keep going. What about the job?" Brielle urged.

"Okay, so it's a really good opportunity, but uh, it's in New York..."

"New York? You know what, you bitches got me feelin' like I went to sleep and woke up in the Middle East with all these bombs you're droppin' today!" Brielle gasped while throwing her hands up in the air.

"Shut your ass up!" I said before tossing my neck back with laughter. "But yeah, I'd be the director of operations at a new office they are opening up in New York."

Brielle shot me a warm smile before turning the champagne bottle back up to her lips. "Ain't nothin' wrong with new beginnings."

"I know, I know."

"How soon would you have to go?" Shauna asked.

"They are giving me ninety days to find a place and relocate."

"You nervous?" Lauryn jumped in.

"Extremely! Cali is my home, you know? But at the same time, like Bri already said, it's a new beginning."

"All I wanna know is if New York is closer to Kansas than Cali is, or further away?" Shauna asked. "Y'all know I barely passed geography back in middle school."

We all burst out into tears of laughter, falling back against the soft pink, plush pillows under the cabana. "I'm not sure, but why does that matter exactly? It's not like things are really anything between us right now."

"So you gon' sit here and tell me you haven't already calculated the air miles? Oh, aight," Lauryn said, calling my bluff.

I rolled my eyes for the millionth time. "There you go! What more do y'all want from me? I told the man I loved him, and he basically told me to work on myself."

"He ain't wrong. Sometimes, we all need somebody else to hold up the mirror for us to realize our own missteps," Lauryn replied.

"So wait, you *are* in love with him?" Brielle asked, cocking her head to the side. "I mean, I knew you were a fan of the D, but I didn't know things had gotten deeper."

I sighed. "I am, but to be honest, seeing those photos and hearing what y'all had to say on top of what complete strangers had to say, sent me spiraling into survival mode. I just feel like I need to proceed with caution with my heart right now, okay? Can y'all just be okay with that?"

"We're fine with it. The question is, are you okay with that?" Shauna questioned.

"Yeah, and you do know it's okay to fall in love with the wrong people sometimes, right? We've all done it. And I'm not saying falling in love with Hendrix was a bad thing or that he's the wrong person, but you gotta learn to be gentle with yourself," Lauryn added.

"Nah. Fool me once shame on you. That's it. You don't get to fool me twice. I'm good," I told them all.

Shauna frowned. "So what do you do with all the feelings you accumulate, besides tuck them under the pillow of the next nigga you hop on?"

Brielle's closed lips spread wide across her face as she turned away from me and mumbled, "Damn. That was a whole read."

"Whatever. Y'all know I've always been like this. I don't need a mothafucka that don't need me, and once I'm off you, I'm off you," I defended, looking down to rotate the stack rings on my fingers.

Shauna's dreads shook from left to right. "Your ass has gotten way too comfortable with sayin' goodbye to niggas and running away from your feelings is a race you'll never win, boo."

I ran my tongue along the front of my teeth before parting my lips to speak. "Who says I'm running?"

"Girl, what? Your track star ass stay running away from the good and running straight to the bullshit," Shauna declared, continuing to call me out.

My eyes shifted downward to my ankle as I wound it in circles. "I guess some old habits die hard."

"You said it yourself, he checks all your boxes, right?" Brielle confirmed.

"Yeah, and?"

"So, stop being childish and go get your man, Cassidy! People are gonna talk shit regardless, but if you believe him when he says that he ain't know that bitch, then nobody else's opinion should matter," Brielle continued.

Lauryn dipped her head in a nod. "Mmhm, including ours."

"But the question is, do you believe him?" Shauna inquired.

"I didn't at first, but I'm not sure if whether I believe him or not even matters at this point."

"Has he ever lied to you before?" Brielle added.

"I'm sure he has in some capacity, right? Niggas lie all the time. It's practically embedded in their DNA."

"Yeah, sure. but what if he wasn't lying about this?"

"Damn, you mean I slapped that nigga for no reason?" Lauryn asked, cocking her head to the side.

"Hold up, you what? When did you see him to slap him?"

"Girl, I slapped the dog shit out his ass for what he did to you, in my dreams, though girl. I was tearing his ass up, too! Ain't nobody going to get away with embarrassing my blood! You know I'm 'bout it, 'bout it!"

I chuckled. "You know I appreciate your crazy, pregnant ass, right?"

Lauryn shot me a face-splitting grin. "But for real, Cass. You need to take a good look in the mirror and ask yourself what you really want. If it's him, great. But if it's not, you gotta be okay with that, too."

As hard it was to sit there and take everything my girls threw at me, it was what I needed to hear. "You're right. You all are right. And I think maybe that's why things are aligning for me the way they are right now."

"So, it sounds like you're moving to New York, huh?" Brielle asked.

"Yup. Looks like I am," I confirmed.

Shauna raised the glass of Moscato she had in hand. "Well, congratulations, girl."

"Look at us, y'all! We've got new jobs, new promotions, new houses, marriages and shit! Life may feel like some bullshit most days, but it's days like this that I feel like things are really going to turn out great for all of us," Lauryn cheered.

———

Two glasses of wine and an additional hour of girl talk later, I hugged Lauryn one last time before heading to the front door.

"Yo, Cass. Long time, no see," Lauryn's brother, Mark, announced, approaching me from the right.

"Mark, hey. I was meaning to get over to you and say hey, but that sister of yours has been working me like a slave since I got here this morning," I said, letting my hand slip away from the doorknob.

"It's all good. I already know what's up with her crazy ass. How you been, fam?"

"You know me, just hanging in there. Making moves when I can make them," I said illusively. "How are you?"

"Shit, I'm out here doin' the same thing. You spoke to Hendrix lately?"

"Are we really gonna stand here and act like the two of you don't talk as much as Lauryn and I do? I already know you know what went down between us."

"Yeah, I do. You good?

I shrugged. "I'm...processing."

"Look, I know I shouldn't even be tellin' you this, but you family, so I'ma do it," he said.

"Telling me what?"

"That nigga was sick over that shit when it first went down. I ain't never seen him like that over nobody he's ever dated, not even his ex, Carina."

"Mmm," I said, mashing my lips together at the mere mention of his ex's name.

"He even tried to get his teammate to call you up and tell you the truth."

"What? He never told me that."

"Because I talked his ass out of it, that's why. Like I said, I don't even know why I'm tellin' you this shit. All this is goin' against the code, but I know you a good woman, and he's a good dude. I just wanna see good people doing good shit together, that's all."

I dipped my head in a silent nod. My conversation with Mark did nothing but prove once again, I'd mishandled everything about Hendrix, including his heart. A puff of air burst past my lips. "Thanks for letting me know."

"I mean, I know it's none of my business and both of y'all grown and all, but I know he'd be happy to hear from you."

"Thanks," I acknowledged. "Well uh, I got a little bit of a drive ahead of me, so I'm going to get on the road. It was nice seeing you."

"You too, fam," he piped before pulling me into a quick hug and sending me on my way.

I gave into the adrenaline rush coursing through my veins as soon as my body was privately confined inside my car and called Hendrix.

The phone rang four times before I heard shouting, banging, and cheering on the other end of the phone.

"H—hello?" Hendrix answered.

My heart practically leapt out of my chest as butterflies danced through my abdomen. "H—hey. Uh, did I catch you at a bad time?"

"Nah, this just locker room shit. We just came off another win. Niggas is hype in here."

"Congratulations! Today was Lauryn's baby shower, so I didn't get a chance to tune in," I admitted.

"It's all good. Your boy handled the roc like a God out there on the court today," he boasted.

I smiled at the recollection of how he used to handle all my curves like a pro. Just the sound of his deep voice had turned my insides upside down. "I bet."

"You good though? I can barely hear you."

"Oh, uh yeah, I didn't want anything, really. I uh, wanted to let you know that I was offered the job. You know, the one I thought I bombed the interview for?"

"See! What I tell you? I knew you had that shit in the bag! Congrats, Cass. Nobody deserves it more than you do."

I grinned. "Thank you."

"You're welcome."

"There's just one thing though…"

"What?"

"It's in New York," I informed him.

"New York? Wow. How you feel about that?"

"I'm sure I'll probably go through my fair share of separation anxiety at first, but I think I'll eventually find my footing there."

"Yeah, I know you'll be fine."

"I have to give them my decision next week, and then I have to find a place and relocate in the next ninety days."

"I got a boy who's a licensed realtor out there. I can shoot him your number if you want and have him see what's available for you."

"You'd do that for me?"

"I'd do anything for you, Cass."

I chewed my bottom lip for a second. "I just thought that because of Christmas, and—"

"I meant everything I said to you that day, but I don't hate you."

"I'ma pass him your number. Give him a few days to reach out. Aight?"

"Yeah, um sure. Thanks."

"No problem."

"Speaking of real estate...I still have the key to your place, you know?"

"I know. What about it?"

"Nothing...I just didn't know if you still wanted me to keep it or mail it back to you somehow."

"If I didn't want you to have it, I never would've given it to you in the first place."

"So, you want me to just...?" I asked, nervously tightening my hand around the steering wheel.

"Hold onto it, Cass. I ain't goin' nowhere."

"Are you sure?"

"Yeah," he assured me.

The words *I miss you, Hendrix* wanted to jump off my lips so bad, but I wouldn't let them. Instead, I said, "Cool, well, I'll let you get back to celebrating. Congrats again."

"Thanks, Cass. Congrats again to you, too."

I ended the call and tossed my head back against the headrest. "Fuck," I mumbled. "I'm really moving to New York," I whispered to myself, knowing come Monday morning, the job would officially be mine.

eight

. . .

Three months later

CASSIDY

"Jameson passes it out to Mitchell, and then back inside to Croft for the step back. It's Croft for three, and it's good!"

"Here's Jackson with the rebound. He's driving it down the court and to the basket for two."

"The ball ricochets to Brooks, who passes it to Croft. He's moving back down the court with such precision. And it's a slam dunk, baby!"

The sports commentators continued to provide background noise in my bedroom, giving a play-by-play of the game Hendrix played against Detroit. With my Egyptian cotton towel wrapped tightly around my body, I carried myself from my bathroom and into my closet to pull out my suitcase. With one quick tug, I tossed it on top of my bed and cracked it open to start packing for my trip to Miami for a tech conference I was speaking at in a few days.

I'd always be a Cali girl at heart, but over the past three months, I had really started to find my groove in New York. Hendrix's realtor friend had come through, and I got to call a brand new two-bedroom apartment with a view from the thirty-second floor my new home on the Upper East Side. I'd halfway figured out how to navigate the subway system, and I'd found a good takeout spot a few blocks away from my building with the best cheesecake I'd ever had in my life. Aside from getting accustomed to new responsibilities at work, I'd spent my time in the city that 'never sleeps' getting both my new place and my fragile heart in order. As I started on my true journey of healing, I let the words of my girls and Hendrix soak in, only to realize that I was passing off the broken, unhealed version of myself as something more complete than what I was.

My laundry list of failed relationships and underlying current of insecurity had created a festering wound that I never took the time out to properly nurse. I slapped a band-aid over it and kept moving. Truthfully, my heart still hadn't processed the magnitude of damage Omar caused, and then I allowed Hendrix to come in and take the battered and scarred pieces that were left. So, I cut both dating and sex from my diet completely and awarded myself with time to grow and heal until I felt I could come correct. When that time came, the only person I was going to step to was Hendrix Croft. I wanted to make sure I had nothing but harvested positive energy to give to him because it was what he deserved most.

I swiped up the remote and turned the TV volume down when I heard the factory iPhone ringtone. "Hey, girl," I answered for Lauryn.

"Hey, lady. What are you doin'?"

"Just got out of the shower not too long ago," I said, plopping down on my side of the bed. "What about you? How's mommy life treating you? I can't believe I still haven't gotten the chance to fly out and meet little miss Bleu yet. These FaceTime calls ain't cuttin' it. I want all the baby cuddles!"

"It's...fuckin' nothin' like I thought it would be. All she does is piss and shit and throw up all day. And then has the nerve to not wanna go to sleep. Like, sis, chill. You ain't missin' nothin' out in these streets," she complained.

I could hear the irritability from lack of sleep in her voice. "Oh, the joys of motherhood."

"You gon' find out one day, trust."

I cocked my head to the side. "You have to have sex to get pregnant, remember?"

She chuckled. "Shit, not these days."

"Have Brielle or Shauna been by?"

"They both have on separate occasions, but you know Bri is starting her new job in Sacramento next week, so she's been trying to get settled."

"I hear that. I still have boxes stuffed in the corner frowning at me," I admitted.

"Shauna's ass came by just before she headed to the airport."

I smacked my turned-up lips. "That hoe ain't tell me she was going out of town when I talked to her last."

"Hell yeah. She's on the move, move! Talkin' 'bout she need a six-month vacation twice a year." She giggled.

I belted out a quick laugh. "I know that's right. I'm with her on that! I'd give anything to be laid up on somebody's beach right now. That's exactly what I plan to do at least one of these days I'm in Miami," I babbled, before getting up to toss my bikini into my suitcase.

"Um, excuse me? Miami? What exactly do you have planned this weekend? Why wasn't I invited?" She pouted.

"Chill. It's all work, and little to no play. I'm speaking at a tech conference there on Thursday. I'm actually trying to pack a few things right now."

"Oh wee! Look at you! My bitch is headlining business conferences and shit now! Okay! I see you!"

"Chill, I'm far from the headliner, but it's still pretty dope," I acknowledged.

"Dope, indeed."

I distractedly sidled down the hallway and over to the oversized window in the living room taking in the 360-degree view of the city. "Yeah…"

"So…" Lauryn probed.

"What?"

"I heard the game on in the background…when's the last time you spoke to you know who?"

I rolled my eyes, knowing exactly who she was referring to. "Maybe a week or two ago. Not really sure." I shrugged.

Although I was taking a much-needed break from men, my soul still *missed* Hendrix like no other. He checked in from time to time, or I would reach out to congratulate him on a win or offer a kind word or two after a loss, but we'd had no physical contact. Not even a Face-Time call.

"Not really sure, huh?"

I lied before turning my attention back to the screen to watch him dribble the ball as his shoes screeched down the glossy court. "Nope. But uh, I do know he'll be in Miami the same time as me. So, who knows, maybe we'll cross paths."

"And then will you finally give up this cheesy ass vow of celibacy and let that nigga break yo' back for old times' sake?"

I snicked. "If it'll make you happy, I'll think about it."

"Yes, it would make me ecstatic to know somebody done took the stick out your ass and put it in a better spot," she joked.

We both let out roar after roar of laughter before they were drowned out by the sound of a very unhappy baby who was either hungry, wet, or a combination of the two.

Lauryn smacked her teeth. "But nah, Cass—I'm glad you're taking the time you need to get right with yourself."

"Thank you."

"But let me go tend to the princess. You know I gotta jump when she say jump, or shit gets real around here."

"Oh, you ain't know Miss Bleu runs shit now?"

"She's a serious boss baby and can't walk or talk yet."

"If she's anything like you then you're in for a crazy ride for the next eighteen years."

"Pray for me, girl."

I put my hands up. "I got you girl, black prayer hands and all," I promised her.

"Bye, Cass."

"Later, girl."

———

I touched down in Miami Thursday evening and headed straight to my hotel room at the Fontainebleau in South Beach. I'd been to Miami a handful of times in the past and nothing compared to it. From the breathtaking views of the ocean to the comfortable beds, it screamed luxury. After stepping out of the shower, I wrapped myself in the plush bathrobe and stepped out onto my private balcony and took in the beautiful view of the sun setting against the ocean's horizon. My feet topped the railing as my hands naturally found themselves underneath my robe and roaming across my body like nomads.

With my eyes slammed shut, I slid one hand in between my thighs while the other massaged my breasts. The combination of the soft fabric and warm evening breeze felt soothing against my freshly washed skin and made my nipples get harder and harder. My mouth gaped open as I slowly rubbed my pussy in slow circles while imagining my fingers were Hendrix's. Although my heart and body had gone on hiatus, they were both still in his possession. I craved his touch so much that I thought about him every time I made myself cum.

"Mmm shit," I moaned as I pressed my fingertips against the hood of my clit.

Fully into the moment, I untied the robe and exposed my fully naked body underneath. I licked my fingertips and slipped two fingers inside me as I imagined his panty-dropping voice whispering all the dirty things he wanted to do to me.

"Fuck!" I squealed.

Cream gushed against my fingertips as I slid them in and out me. I spread my legs wide and hiked my leg back to get the most out of my private pussy play session. My eyes tore down to my glistening pussy as I continued strumming my fingers against my clit like a guitar.

"Oh shit! Oh shit! I'm cumming," I moaned as I thrusted forward against my fingers.

My back arched out of the chair as I squeezed my thighs together to brace myself for a spine-tingling orgasm. After cumming, I left the robe hanging over the balcony railing and skated back inside to grab my vibrator and finish what my fingers had started.

The next morning, I found myself dressed and enjoying my morning coffee on the same cozy lounge chair I'd finger-fucked myself to the evening prior. With my mug in one hand and presentation notes in the other, I went over all my key talking points.

"Good morning and thank you all for joining today's session. My name is Cassidy Stokes, and—*fuck*," I mumbled when my phone rang.

I quickly glanced down at the screen to see my mother calling and answered the phone with aggravation in my greeting. "Hey."

"Cassidy?"

Knowing we were on opposite sides of the country, I glanced down at my watch to check what time it was. "Mom, it's like six o'clock in the morning over there. Why are you calling me so early?" I quizzed.

"There's something I need to tell you."

I rolled my eyes, knowing how dramatic she could be at times. "Can it wait? I'm kind of in the middle of trying to get in the right headspace. I'm in Miami giving a presentation at a conference in like an hour and a half."

"Okay. Call me back then."

"Okay."

"Cassidy Jhene Stokes, I'm serious. Call me back, please."

The *please* at the end of her sentence sent a twinge to my heart. Dr. Angelique Stokes almost never asked for anything, let alone grace.

"I will," I assured, "just let me get through this presentation."

———

Two hours after my presentation, I managed to slip away from the conference and took an Uber to the design district to buy myself a "job well done" gift from the Gucci store. After swiping my Visa, Jonathan, my client advisor, boxed and bagged up my new handbag and handed it to me.

"Thank you so much for visiting us today, Ms. Stokes. Please come back and see me again," he piped with a wink.

A smile swung free as I headed out of the store while pulling out my phone. His mention of my last name reminded me that I needed to call my mother back. I put my AirPods in my ear and waited for her to answer.

She stammered when she answered. "H—hello?"

"Mom?"

"Hey…"

"Is now a good time? You wanted me to call you back to tell me something, remember?"

"Y—yeah."

"But you sound tired like I caught you in the middle of a nap or something. What's wrong with your voice?" I questioned.

She cleared her throat. "Cassidy."

"Yeah?"

"I have stage three breast cancer."

Her words made me freeze in the middle of the street. "W—what?"

"I'm sorry to spring it on you like this, but I figured you needed to know."

"How long have you known?"

"I found out a little before you moved to New York."

My brows heightened in surprise. "And you're just now telling me? Why would you wait this long to tell me something so important?"

"I wasn't sure if you'd care."

I dropped my lower lip in a pout as tears stung my eyes. "What? Why wouldn't I care? You're my mother."

"And you've reminded me time and time again about how much of a bad one I was to you. I just never wanted to admit it."

I lowered my eyes to the ground, unable to stop the millions of thoughts racing through my head. "We can talk about this in person. I'm going to book a flight to you tonight!"

"No, no. You stay right where you are. You don't need to come here. Nothing will change, and I don't need you here putting your life on pause for mine."

"I have so many questions. What are the doctors saying? Did you get a second opinion? Can they operate to remove it? Do you need chemo? Radiation?" I asked before recovering my breath.

She sighed. "Cassidy, slow down."

"I can't, Mom! You just told me you have cancer! I'm losing my mind over here and you're telling me that I can't come see you!"

"I know this is a lot to process."

"Why would you wait until I moved all the way across the country to tell me something like this?"

"Because I knew if there was still a chance that you did care, you'd never leave California."

"Exactly!"

"And I couldn't have that," she reminded me.

Feeling defeated, I aimed my steps at the closest bench I could find and plopped down. "I feel like a terrible person for not knowing. At the end of the day, you're still my mother. I'm sorry—I should've checked in with you more."

"How could you have possibly known something like this would happen? This is exactly why I don't want you here. You can't but my burdens on your shoulders, Cassidy. All I need you to do is promise me that you'll go get yourself checked out."

I bobbed my head up and down while patting the base of my hand against my dewy cheeks. "I will, I promise. I'll make an appointment as soon as I get back to New York."

"Good."

"So, tell me what's going on. I want to know everything," I probed as calmy as my wrecked nerves would allow.

"Well, the good news is the cancer hasn't spread to my organs, and I've been doing an aggressive chemo regimen for months. The doctors keep telling me that if we stick to the treatment plan, there's a good possibility that I can beat it."

"That's a good thing! That's great news!" I quaked as a wave of relief washed over me.

"Yeah, but there is also a high risk that it could come back."

"Well, we're not going to even speak that into existence. Positive vibes only, Mom."

"You're right."

"How are you feeling though?"

"Tired, mostly. Some days I'm sick and don't have much of an appetite, but other than that, I'm managing."

"Managing? You should be doing more than managing. Do you need anything? Are you comfortable? Let me come take care of you," I offered.

"Your Aunt Tina is here every day. She's been helping, and I've hired some help around the house."

"When's your next doctor appointment? I want to be there."

"Cassidy, what did I just say?"

I let out an aggravated sigh. "If you won't let me come see you, let me at least pay to get you more help. Whatever you need, just tell me what you need, Mom," I pleaded, tears springing out of my eyes.

"I need you to keep doing you, Cassidy. I know it may not have seemed like it, maybe ever, but you have made me so proud. You always have. And maybe I didn't know how to show you that, or maybe my guidance and criticism were the worst thing for you and tore you down more than built you up."

"M—mom."

"I just want you to know that I'm sorry," she acknowledged.

I never imagined I would be standing in the middle of a street in Miami when my mother and I would have our 'Come to Jesus' moment, but there we were.

"Cassidy? Did I lose you?" she asked when I didn't respond.

Goosebumps pebbled my arms. "I'm here."

"Did you hear what I said?"

"I did, and I—I guess I don't know what to say because I never knew you were listening."

"I was always listening. I just never wanted to hear you because every time you told me how you were feeling, it was like you were holding up a mirror in my face, and I couldn't take it. So, I let you push me away because I couldn't admit that you were right."

My heartrate still hadn't found a resting beat and the right words still hadn't found their way to my tongue. "Wow, Mom. I—I don't know what to say."

"You've said enough over the years and now it's my turn. After the diagnosis, I started to put a lot of things into perspective. I started finally allowing myself to deal with the death of your father."

Hearing her news had me wondering how I would deal with losing another parent after losing my father six years prior. "I'm glad you're trying to work on yourself, Mom."

"Gotta do it while I still have breath in my body to do so, right?"

"Yeah."

"Listen, I didn't mean to bring down your day with all my sad news. How did your presentation go?" she questioned, changing the subject.

The uptick in her voice made me smile for the first time during our conversation. "It went good. I got a lot of good feedback after."

"I knew it would. I'm so, so proud of you, Cassidy."

"Thank you."

"But listen, your aunt just got here, so I'm going to talk to you later, okay?"

"I'll call you tomorrow."

"Sounds good."

I hung up the phone and sat dumbfounded. It would have been impossible to try and process everything my mother had just told me right then and there. After making sure my eyes were dry, I glided past a store with my nose in my phone, trying to find a good meeting point for my Uber to pick up me and take me back to my hotel. I was no longer in the mood for retail therapy.

"Cassidy?"

I froze before turning around, allowing my mind time enough to process the male voice that had called out to me. "Omar?"

nine

. . .

CASSIDY

I turned to see Omar Devante Greyson's pecan brown eyes staring back at me. I was sure I still looked visibly upset, but I tried my best to hide it. I always envisioned that the moment we crossed paths again would be a day of reckoning. Yet, I was puffy-eyed and snot-nosed, just how I was the last time he'd seen me.

"You good?" he asked, assessing my mood and snapping me out of my twisted fantasy at the same time.

"Me? Yeah, I'm good."

"Yeah? Life treatin' you good?"

"Yeah. You?"

"Same. It's crazy running into you here. What are you doin' out in Miami?"

"Work conference," I answered, keeping my responses short.

"Oh, cool."

"And what about you? You're a little far from Tallahassee, right?"

"I am. We made the move out here a couple months ago."

I dipped my head in a quick nod while driving my eyes past him. "Cool. Listen, it was nice seeing—"

"Cass, wait. I didn't expect to see you again, let alone today. I told myself that if I ever did cross paths with you again, I'd tell you to your face that I'm sorry for how I handled everything. I don't regret my son, but you never deserved to be tangled up in any of that."

I couldn't deal with everyone who had a place in my heart, whether past or present, using me as their emotional sounding board. My emotions were already running high after finding out about my mother's diagnosis, and a part of me fought to respond with something toxic, but I refrained from saying anything that would keep us in each other's presence longer than need be.

"Listen Omar, I—"

He interjected before I could finish, "And I know that shit just probably made everything awkward, but I had to get it off my chest."

I shook my head. "This entire conversation is awkward, Omar. It's fine. It's been months. We've both moved on," I said, stating fact over fiction.

No sooner than the words fell off my lips, his phone lit up, showcasing a family photo of the three of them and she had a ring on her finger. It was then that I realized that Omar was more of a stepping-stone to me than he was a stumble. He'd come into my life for a season. Long enough for me to teach his ass a thing or two before he could go back to her and be the man she required, which wasn't the man I needed. Seeing him again only made me realize just how special Hendrix was. For once, I was the project, and he was the fixer.

"I'm glad it all worked out for you, really…" I told him.

"Yeah, same for you and that ball player," he mentioned.

Although he hadn't mentioned Hendrix by name, my antennas went up. "How'd you even know anything about that? I thought you weren't into the blogs and celeb gossip."

"I'm not. Malaya, she saw and mentioned it."

"Mentioned it, huh?" I asked. *I would've like to have been a fly on the wall for that conversation*, I thought to myself.

"Yeah, and I mean to be honest, I was like *damn, she traded up from a nigga like me*. I knew you deserved better than me, Cass. We both did. That ain't no secret."

Correct, I thought.

"I ain't have my shit together when you met me, and I wasn't ready for someone like you."

Also correct, I thought.

He licked his pink lips before speaking up again. "He keepin' you happy, right?"

My eyes brightened with relief when I looked past him to see my driver in the gray Toyota Corolla pulling up in the nick of time. I was not about to talk to my old nigga about my *new*, old nigga.

"My Uber is here, so I gotta go. Take care of yourself," I said before slipping into the backseat of the sedan and pulling off.

ten

· · ·

HENDRIX

I was in Miami conditioning on a workout bike with the team a few hours before the game. ESPN blared on every TV within the training facility, and I zoned out to catch the tail end of the conversation between the on-air commentators.

"You know what game I can't wait for? The Miami and Kansas City game tonight. I cannot wait to see what Croft is gonna do!"

"You and everybody else, Roland. Croft has been on everybody's radar this season, that's for sure."

"Watching him out there on the court, you would never know he was taken out at the end of last season with a knee injury. The boy gets buckets, Carrie!" Roland hailed.

"I'll admit it does seem like Croft can do no wrong. Kansas City is on fire right now with a four-game winning streak. That's record breaking for the team in general."

"I'm telling you, Carrie, Croft is exactly what the doctor ordered! He brought a team that was on life support back to life! Dare I say MVP?"

"That's it, Roland. I think you're calling it."

I'd be lying if I said I didn't appreciate the past due recognition after niggas counted me out when I got injured and then traded. Most days, I felt like I was carrying the world on my shoulders, so the praise was an internal win. As much as I was against the trade at first, putting the Kansas City jersey on my back was the best career decision I ever made, but I still had a lot to prove. Shaking off their admiration, I put the focus back on my workout. After getting off the bike, I headed to see the team trainer to get stretched out and put my compression knee sleeve on.

"Yo, Croft. Coach Jackson wants to see you in the hallway," my teammate, Sean, told me.

I issued into the hallway and set out for the coach who stood at the end of the hallway talking to a man I'd only heard of in passing, the team owner. "You wanted to see me, Coach?" I asked.

"Croft, I'd like you to meet Mitchell West, the Kansas City Titans' team owner."

I reached out my hand to shake his. "Nice to meet you, sir."

"Croft, the pleasure is all mine! I'm excited to be here tonight. It's gonna be a big game. I've heard the entire arena is sold out tonight. How are you feeling?"

"I'm good. Just tryna get in the right headspace and get focused."

"Let's walk," he suggested. We left Coach Jackson behind and took over conversation out to the secluded court. "I wanted to check in to see how you were adjusting so far this season. I mean, by your stats, you're doing great, but I wanted to personally check in."

"I'm proud to be a Titan, and I appreciate the fresh start. I'm trying to stay the course, have a successful season, and hopefully bring a championship to the city."

He patted my shoulder. "That's good to hear. As you know, the Titans have been chasing a championship for years, and up until you got here, that dream seemed impossible. Now, I feel like it's right at the tip of our fingertips. Fans are calling you the King of Kansas City."

I exchanged a glance with him before flashing a quick grin. "I'm definitely feeling the attention and the pressure," I assured him.

He spoke quickly, "I'm not sure if you know this or not, but we moved heaven and earth to acquire you and you've made us very proud. I'm excited to see what else you can do."

I understood the hierarchy in the league and for that reason, I sunk my teeth into my bottom lip to avoid saying the first thing that came to mind. I was never one to shy away from praise, but he was talking to me as if I was a show pony or some prized exotic breed of dog.

"Thank you. All I can do is go out there and play the game I wanna play."

"You have a bright career ahead of you. If you keep doing what you're doing, you'll rule this entire franchise, son. Just something to think about," he said, patting my shoulder again. "If there's anything you need or that we can do for you, don't. hesitate to ask."

I bobbed my head as I noticed a few of my teammates heading out onto the court. "Thank you. I'm about to go do shoot around with the team. Enjoy the game, sir."

"I'm sure I will."

———

An hour and a half after the game ended, I was out in the club celebrating our win with team when my phone vibrated. I looked down and saw *Cass* displayed across the screen. Things had been hanging in the balance between Cassidy and I for months. I'd given her the time to heal and focus on herself, while I focused on my game, but I counted down the days until I could see her again. Instead of answering and struggling to hear her over the loud music, I opted to text her.

> Me [11:42 p.m.]: I'm out celebrating with the team. Sup?

> Cass [11:43 p.m.]: Congrats on another win...

> Me [11:43 p.m.]: Thank you.

Three ellipses showed up and then disappeared multiple times. Just as I went to shove the phone back in my pocket, she hit me back.

Cass [11:47 p.m.]: I was wondering if we could talk…

Me [11:49 p.m.]: About?

Cass [11:53 p.m.]: Us.

Me [11:54 p.m.]: When?

Cass [11:55 p.m.]: Tonight. I'm in Miami.

Me [11:57 p.m.]: When were you gon' tell me that?

Cass [11:59 p.m.]: I wasn't sure if you would want to see me. It's been a min.

Me [12:02 a.m.]: I always wanna see you, Cass. Where you stayin'?

Cass [12:03 a.m.]: The Fontainebleau. Room 3413.

Me [12:07 a.m.]: Bet. I'm about to pull up on you.

I said my goodbyes to my boys and swanned through the club to wait for the valet to bring my car around. As much as I knew I should've stayed to continue celebrating with my team, Cassidy had more of a hold over me than she thought. Something inside me craved her energy, no matter which way she was coming with it, and I had to see her. My body slid behind the seat of the Mercedes I'd rented to get around for the few days I was in the city, and I headed to see her. With five minutes left until I arrived at her hotel, I stopped at a red light where traffic was a little backed up. I glanced down at my phone for a second and then up in time to see a black and orange Kawasaki motorcycle crash into the back of me, and then everything went black.

eleven

. . .

HENDRIX

I woke up to the dim overhead light softly bouncing off the four pale walls around me. My cold hand gripped the side rail as I slowly sat myself up to look around the private hospital room I'd ended up in. My thoughts were foggy. The last thing I remembered was seeing the motorcycle getting closer and closer before impact and then, nothing. The blood pressure cuff around my right arm started to hum and squeeze my arm until it went numb. My eyes continued to scan the dimly lit room until they landed on Cassidy. She was curled up and sleeping in the recliner chair right next to the metal IV stand I was connected to.

"Cass?" I mumbled as I ran my tongue over my chapped lips.

She stirred instantly at the sound of my voice and quickly popped her eyes open. "Hendrix? You're awake!"

"What happened?" I asked, licking my lips again.

"Oh, here," she said, shooting up to put a straw up to my lips so I could take a sip of water.

My eyes oscillated around as I sipped. The blinds were closed to keep out shots of the press and paparazzi trying to get their next scoop. "Thank you."

"Do you remember anything from the accident?"

"Some, but not everything. I must've blacked out when the airbags deployed. I remember seeing a black and orange motorcycle coming up behind me and not stopping. Then, I woke up here."

"Yeah, you were in an accident. The police said that the motorist lost control of the motorcycle trying to avoid the backed-up traffic and crashed right into you. They transported you to a local hospital to run some tests, do some X-rays, and ensure you didn't have a concussion or reinjure your knee."

"My knee?" I said, instantly reaching down to rub it.

"Don't worry. Your X-rays came back fine. Your knee is fine. They just want to keep you overnight for observation, so they gave you some medicine to help you rest and help with some of the soreness from the accident."

"What about the guy on the bike?"

She lowered her head. "He died at the scene."

My mouth hung open for a brief second. I didn't know how to feel. On the one hand, a life had been lost, but on the other, I was relieved to know someone else's carelessness hadn't shattered my career. I pushed the stiff white starched bleach white sheets off me and slowly threw my feet over the edge of the bed. My muscles were definitely sore, but I was happy to hear that I hadn't reinjured my knee.

"How'd you know I was here?" I inquired.

"It's all over the news."

"Then, how'd you manage to get back here with all the coverage?"

"One of the nurses spotted my face from those pictures on those damn blogs and let me back."

I chuckled. "Dare I say the paparazzi can be useful sometimes?"

She smirked. "Barely. But how are you feeling? Are you in any pain? Do you need anything?"

"I'm good. To be honest, I'm shocked to see you here. Happy, but shocked."

"If I've learned anything over the past twenty-four hours, it's that life is way too short," she admitted.

"Yeah, it is."

"I uh, I found out my mom has stage three breast cancer," she confessed.

My eyebrows jutted in shock. "Damn. I'm sorry to hear that. How you dealin' with that? You aight?"

She shrugged. "I don't know what I am, honestly. We talked and she actually apologized for all her years of criticism, and it was just…a lot. It just sucks that it took something tragic to happen to force her to have the conversation I've been trying to have for years."

"Better late than never, right?"

"Exactly, and that's why I wanted to talk to you. I didn't want any more time to pass between us before I told you how I feel."

"Okay. I'm listenin'."

Her chest caved with an exhale. "You know for the past few months, I've been trying to get my shit in order because I heard what you said to me on Christmas. I heard you loud and clear, and I realized that taking out my ex's sins on you wasn't fair, and I never apologized to you for that. I was too caught up trying to be the victim in the situation. I was hurt and I was angry, and I let my insecurities eat away at me and…I just wasn't ready for a nigga like you," she admitted.

Her vulnerability was refreshing to say the least. "And what about now?" I asked, reaching out to grab her hands.

"What?"

"Are you ready for a nigga like me now?"

She flashed her eyes up at me with a disarming stare. "I wrote your name on my heart and it's there to stay," she responded.

"And do you trust that it's safe with me?"

"I do."

"Why?"

"Why what?"

"Why do you trust that it's safe with me?"

"Because as much as I've tried to fight it, I'm in love with you, Hendrix. Maybe a part of me always has been since we were teenagers, I don't know. All I know is that there's something in me that needs you. I just need to know that you need me too."

Cassidy had bewitched my soul months ago in St. Martin. Time had passed, but nothing had changed on my end. My heart was all hers. "Baby, I've been without you for months, and I don't want to be without you for a second longer," I said, pulling her into my arms.

twelve

· · ·

CASSIDY

Hendrix and I left the hospital together the next day hand-in-hand and unbothered about what anyone had to say about it. I was grateful that aside from a few scrapes and sore muscles, he was perfectly fine and was cleared to fly back to Kansas City and play in his next game. When we got back to his hotel room, I sauntered up to Hendrix as he placed himself on the edge of the couch and pulled me to him to kiss my stomach through my shirt. "I'm glad you're here," he admitted as his hands cradled the dip of my waist.

He laid his head against my stomach before looking down and kissing my pussy through my jeans. My thighs hugged each other, trying to suppress the throbbing of my love maker. I missed the feeling of his body against mine. For months, I'd envisioned the things I wanted to do to him. *Filthy shit. Vile, even.*

"Hendrix," I breathed. It was impossible to keep my head on straight when I was around him.

"You want me to stop?" he asked, kissing it again.

"No," I answered.

"Tell me what you want, Cass," he said, standing to his full stature.

I flashed my eyes up at him and locked my fingers in his beard before standing on the tips of my toes to place a kiss on his lips. "I want you inside me, Hendrix," I panted, unable to hold a poker face.

I stepped out of his grasp and took off my clothes piece by piece. He leaned back and watched as I tossed everything to the floor until there was nothing left but a set of hard nipples and a smile.

"Come to Daddy, baby."

I straddled his lap and pulled his shirt over his head. My hands roamed over his hardening dick that was threatening to bust through his jeans. I tugged at his belt, urging him to pull his pants down so I could take my seat on his ten-inch throne. He kissed me deeply, letting his tongue do backflips in my mouth as I slowly slid down every inch.

"Oooh shit," I squealed, sucking in air and biting down on his lip.

"Mmm," he groaned in my ear.

Hendrix's large hands absorbed my hips before sliding down to spread my ass cheeks apart. I slithered up and down his pole like a stripper as my fingertips danced in my scalp. "Goddamn, I missed you."

"Mmm, you love this dick?"

"I do. I fuckin' do," I purred.

"Tell me how much you missed me."

"I missed you so much, baby," I whispered against his kissable mouth before gently slicing my teeth into his juicy bottom lip.

He scooted to the edge of the couch and stood up to fuck me suspended in the air. His muscles flexed as he drove my pussy up and down his dick.

Thrusting my bare hips forward, I moaned out, "Yesss! Fuck me just like that, baby!"

Switching positions, Hendrix dropped me onto the bed, grabbed my ankle and flipped me over onto my stomach. All ten inches barged through my walls as he pulled my hair back and whispered all the freaky shit he'd been wanting to do to me in my ear.

I hummed. "Mmm, fuck."

"I missed this pussy. It's mine, right?"

"It's all yours, baby."

"Mmm, shit. Tell me it's mine again, Cass," he coaxed before slipping his bottom lip underneath his front teeth.

His deep voice sounded so fuckin' sexy. I felt a puddle forming underneath me. "It's yours, Hendrix!" I screamed out in pleasure.

He lay his palm flat to my spine, guiding my pussy back to swallow up his dick again and again. "Oooh," I moaned, drawing in a sharp breath.

"That's right. Take that dick, Cass. Take it."

My eyes slickened with lust as I looked over my shoulder at Hendrix, who had hooked his hand across my waist. "Mmm."

"Look at all this cream on my dick. That's all you, baby," he noted.

I licked the palm of my hand before reaching back to stroke his shaft while he simultaneously pushed in and out of me. "Mmm, shit," he growled, "keep my pussy in the air for me and let Daddy taste it."

I stayed propped up on all fours as Hendrix French kissed my pussy before moving up to bury his face in my ass with no questions asked. He slurped and lathered my asshole with spit before sliding a finger inside.

"Ooh shit!" I squealed, clenching the sheets in my hands.

He flipped me over and climbed on top to place kisses down my slender stomach. I fought through my moans of pleasure as his lips spoke in tongues across my body.

"Mmm, it's so wet for me," he said as he ran his hand over my pussy that was as smooth as a fresh coat of paint. "Can I taste it, baby?"

I sat up on my elbows and peered down at him. What he'd done to my insides was a pure violation, and he had yet to truly bless me with his magical tongue game for the night. Instead of responding, I locked eyes with him and pulled my elongated legs back to my shoulders. He sexily bit his bottom lip again before smirking. We both knew what time it was.

He submerged his head between my thighs, growling as his fingertips tugged at my nipples. A raspy moan glided past my slightly parted lips as he firmly pressed his tongue against my clit. Squirming underneath his grasp, I started to wind my hips in a slow circular motion and thrust into his soft lips.

"Mmm, your tongue feels so fuckin' good," I growled, skating my fingers through his hair.

"You gon' cum for Daddy?" he asked, nibbling at the juiciness of my thighs with his beautiful teeth.

"Keep givin' me that fuckin' tongue and I'ma cum for you, Daddy," I guaranteed.

"Mmm," he hummed before flicking the tip of his tongue against my clit like a snake.

"Ahh!" I squealed, inching forward. "Ahh! K—keep it right—right there, baby."

I gripped both sides of his head and slid his lips up and down my sweet spot until the levee broke—instantly sending me into a cumming frenzy. "Ahhhh, fuckkkkkkkk!" I screamed, arching my back to Jehovah himself.

My hips twitched in aftershock as I looked down to see my cream leaking all over his lips and glistening in his beard. He ran his hand down his drenched face and threw my legs back. As soon as he pushed the tip in, I squirted.

"Oooh. Daddy got that pussy gushin' already. Show me how you squirt, baby," he demanded, driving the tip in and out and smacking it against my pussy.

"Oh my God!" I screamed, unable to control my body's jerks and shakes.

The sheets were completely soaked beneath us as Hendrix masked himself back inside my warmth, covering his dick in my cream once again. My arms locked around his neck as he fed me the dick, slowly dipping in and out of my ocean. I opened my eyes to see Hendrix staring back at me with a set of bedroom eyes and a handsome scowl across his face.

"You look so fuckin' beautiful," he said as he slid two fingers inside my watery mouth.

I moaned and sucked them as our bodies converged, one deep stroke after the other. He tossed my leg over his shoulder and kissed my ankle as my fourteen-karat ankle bracelet dangled against my foot. Leaning forward, Hendrix cupped his hand around my throat and kissed me. My eyes rolled back in my head as he thrusted harder inside me.

"I love it when you moan for me," he mumbled against my lips.

My triumphant screams could be heard echoing through the entire hotel room, maybe even the entire floor for all I knew. "Shit, baby! I—I'm cumming. I'm cumming!"

"Fuck, I'm cumming, too," he announced seconds before his body began to jerk with pleasure.

"Mmm, put it in my mouth," I insisted.

"What you say?"

"I said, put it in my mouth, baby."

"You wanna suck all the nut off this dick?"

I nodded. "Mmhm. It's my dick, ain't it?"

"Hell yeah, it's yours," he vowed before sliding his creamy dick out of my lower set of lips and into the top set. I moaned when it touched my tongue.

He gripped a handful of my hair and tossed his head back. "Mmm, shit. Goddamn I love you. Suck all that shit off, baby."

I sucked up the nut and spit it back out on his dick before rubbing it across my lips. "Give it all to me, baby," I said, before letting his dick smack the back of my throat and sliding it back out.

"Shiiiiiiiiiiiitttt." He trembled. "Why the fuck would you do that to me?"

"You needed to know how much I missed all of you," I told him before wiping his seed off my bottom lip.

———

Three weeks later, I was walking through the airport terminal in Kansas City after leaving Cali to get to Hendrix's game. After explaining my mother's health situation with my management, they allowed me to fly back to California for a few weeks and work remotely while I was able to spend time with my mother and get her in a good place before returning to New York. Even though she had a long road ahead of her, I was glad we were finally able to work on our relationship.

I spent the evening jumping up and down in heels and cheering Hendrix and the rest of the team on as they held on to beat Denver. After the game, I ushered out of the arena with everyone else and waited for Hendrix out by his car. An hour and fifteen minutes after the game ended, I was still waiting for him. I'd gone from patient, to slightly annoyed, to all the way bothered in that timespan. After calling his phone for the twentieth time and getting his voicemail, I was about ready to call myself and Uber and leave. As soon as I got up the nerve to open the ride share app, he called me back.

"Hendrix, where are you? I've been waiting for over an hour!" I snapped.

"I know. I'm sorry. Come back inside the arena."

"Come back? Why would I come back inside? The game is over. They probably won't let me back in anyway," I griped.

"Just come back to the front of the arena, Cass. I'll meet you there."

"Why can't you just come out here? My feet are killing me!" I whined as I begrudgingly trekked back to the arena.

My eyelashes glittered with tears the second I pushed through the arena doors and saw what had to have been millions of bright red rose petals leading inside. Eyes fuzzed over with moisture, I looked up to see Hendrix standing there with a bouquet of red roses in hand.

"Hendrix? What is all this?" I asked before my mouth dropped open in awe.

"You like it?"

"Like it? I love it. Everything is so beautiful. How did you even arrange all of this?"

"I called in a favor with someone I know," he answered.

"What are we even doing in here?" I asked, bombarding him with yet another question.

"Just come with me, baby."

He slipped his hand in mine and led the way, following the rose path illuminated with hundreds of tealight candles. The entire arena had been cleared out and it was only the two of us in sight.

"You put all this together, baby?" I quizzed.

He dipped his chin in concession. "Yeah, I did."

"Impressive."

"Best date you've ever been on?"

"Hands down," I said, giving him his just due.

"Good. I wanted tonight to be memorable."

"And why is that? You're not gon' make me play you in no *Love and Basketball* type shit, are you? Because these Dior heels are barely allowing me to walk any further," I notified him.

He let out a soft chuckle. "I don't want to break your ankles, baby. Only your back."

I laughed alongside him as we stepped inside the elevator and went up to the area where the VIP suites were. "Shut up. How much longer do we have to walk?" I asked as we stepped off the elevator.

"We're almost there."

"Don't think I haven't noticed that you still didn't answer my question about what we were doing here," I reminded him.

Hendrix opened the door to a private suite, and we stepped inside. "Why don't you look over there and see."

I prowled forward to get a closer look out of the window and onto the arena floor. The words *Will you marry me* were written across the arena floor in the same red roses that had led us to the suite. I gasped and turned around to see Hendrix down on one knee. The moment he reached out and grabbed my left hand, my thoughts no longer aligned. I'd forgotten my left from my right.

"Cass, letting you walk out of my life again is unacceptable. I knew that the moment I stepped up to you on that plane. You're a smart-mouthed, straight shooter, and exactly what I've been waiting my entire life for. You are the only woman I see being a staple in my life. I want to share forever with you, if you say yes," he voiced, popping open a ring box.

I stood at his feet, tongue-tied and more in love than I'd ever been. Inside was a platinum engagement ring laced with diamonds around the band and a princess cut diamond in the center.

"Oh my God, yes. Yes! Yes! Yes!" I squealed on repeat.

He slid the ring on my finger before standing to his feet and encircling his arms around my waist. "I love you so much."

"I love you, too. Always and forever," I promised before kissing his lips.

. . .

The End.

(Like, seriously, this is the end this time.)

afterword

A note from K.L. Hall

Reader,

Happy holidays! Thank you for reading the highly requested sequel to Cassidy and Hendrix's love story. Please, if you've made it this far, I hope you'll consider taking a minute to tell me what you thought about the book in the form of a **book review and/or rating**. Don't hesitate to let me know what you'd like to see from me next! I thoroughly enjoy reading your reviews and hearing from you as well! I'm always striving to attract new readers and retain current ones, and reviews are one of the easiest ways to attract readers. If you loved the book, tell a friend, and most importantly let me know!

All my love,

K.L. Hall

about the author

As a serial storyteller, K.L. Hall pens enthralling love stories intertwined with the grittiness of urban fiction. Her writing style is a fusion of eminently relatable female characters like Sydney Tate and Raquel Valentine, and the flawed, yet desirable male leads who love them, like Law Calloway and Justice Silva.

Reader Faves:

In the Arms of a Savage: *(Peaked at #1 in Women's Fiction)*

Solace in Seven: *(Peaked at #2 in African American Erotica)*

Awakened: A Paranormal Romance: *(Peaked at #1 in Erotic Science Fiction)*

Sign up for my mailing list to stay up to date with new releases, giveaways, sneak peeks, and more!

Website: https://www.authorklhall.com

also by k.l. hall

Diary of a Hood Princess 1-3

Rise of a Street King: The Justice Silva Story *(Spin-Off to the Diary of a Hood Princess series)*

Where He Belongs: A Disrespectful Love Story

Love Me Harder: A Sin City Love Story

Broken Condoms and Promises 1-3

In the Arms of a Savage 1-3

Built for a Savage: Blaze and Camille's Love Story *(Spin-Off to the In the Arms of a Savage Series)*

A Ruthle$$ Love Story 1-3

Fallin' for the Alpha of the Streets 1-2

The Most Savage of Them All: The Wolfe Calloway Story *(Prequel to the In the Arms of a Savage Series)*

When a Gangsta Loves a Good Girl

Caught Between my Husband and a Hustler

The Illest Taboo 1-2

To the Only Thug I'll Ever Love

Novellas:

Bi-Curious: An Erotic Tale

Bi-Curious 2: Tastes Like Candy

House of Cards 1-2

A Savage Calloway Christmas *(Christmas novella to the In the Arms of a Savage Series)*

Lovin' the Alpha of the Streets: A Valentine's Day Novella *(Valentine's Day novella to the Fallin' for the Alpha of the Streets Series)*

Awakened: A Paranormal Romance

As Long as You Stay Down

Solace in Seven

At Your Best: Solace in Seven Book 2

Children's Books:

Princess for Hire

Princess Twinkle Toes & the Missing Magic Sneakers

Little One, Change the World

Adjust Your Crown: A Self-Love Coloring Book for Children of Color

Non-Fiction:

Authors are a Business: The Booked & Busy Course Mini Book